12/15

398.209 W747s
WILSON
STARS IS GOD'S

D0056045

WITHDRAWN

BK 398.209   W747S
STARS IS GODS LANTERNS; AN OFFERING OF OZARK TELLIN
STORIES
1   C1969   4.95   M   /WILSON, CH

3000 364802 40015
St. Louis Community College

Stars is God's Lanterns

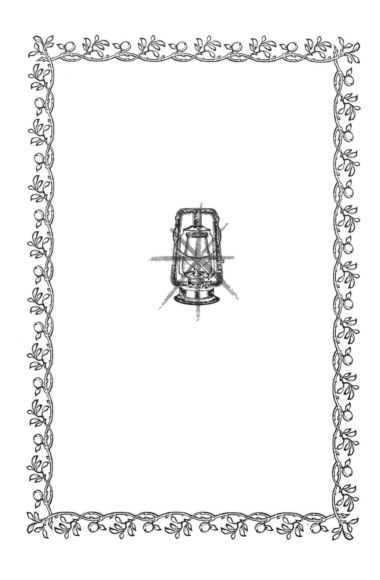

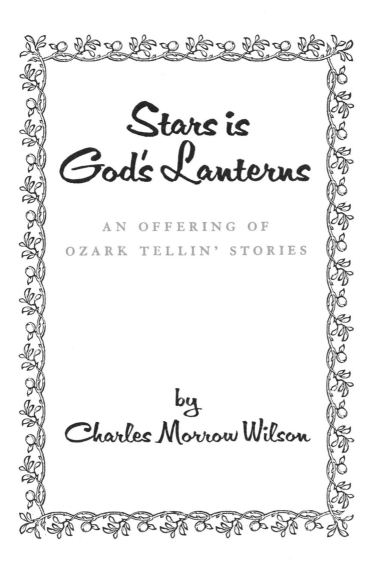

Stars is God's Lanterns

AN OFFERING OF OZARK TELLIN' STORIES

by

Charles Morrow Wilson

SOME RECENT BOOKS BY CHARLES MORROW WILSON

Bodacious Ozarks (New York, 1959)
Let's Try Barter (New York, 1960)
Grass and People (Gainesville, Florida, 1962)
Common Sense Credit (New York, 1962)
Rudolf Diesel: Pioneer of the Age of Power (with W. Robert Nitske)
(Norman, 1965)
Roots: Miracles Below (New York, 1968)
Stars Is God's Lanterns: An Offering of Ozark Tellin' Stories
(Norman, 1969)

.

STANDARD BOOK NUMBER: 8061-0882-7

LIBRARY OF CONGRESS CARD NUMBER: 75-88142

Copyright 1969 by the University of Oklahoma Press, Publishing Division of the University. Composed and printed at Norman, Oklahoma, U.S.A., by the University of Oklahoma Press. First edition.

CONTENTS

Stars is God's Lanterns

MUSING OVERTURE

FOR half a dozen generations the Ozark Mountains of Missouri and Arkansas have been bearing a most exceptional crop—commonly known as tellin' stories. This crop is not necessarily staple or stable. It has deep roots and remarkable pristine integrity. But the species and the harvests are everlastingly in mutation.

Home-grown tellin' stories are of the heritage and indigenous rootage of frontiers. And come good times or bad, hell or high water, Democrats or Republicans, splinters or landslides, the Ozarks remain a frontier.

According to practically any dictionary "frontier" means that part of a country which faces or adjoins other countries or regions that are more densely settled or, forgive the outrageous adjective, "advanced." More certainly definitive of the Ozarks, a frontier is also a realm which is not fully explored in terms of thought, spirit, sentiment, or culture.

The Ozarks tellin' stories provide irrepressible proof of this latter assertion. They are begotten not only by the earth, air, rain, and sunshine of this exceptional region, but by its ill-defended, almost miraculously enduring and invincible spirit.

It isn't easy to substantiate such musings as these. Indeed, it isn't easy to peg down the absolutes of Ozarks geography or geology or anthropology. Stated with some degree of accuracy, the Ozarks comprise a worn-down mountain range fairly close to the middle of the United States mainland. Its total area of about 50,000 square miles includes southwestern Missouri, northwestern Arkansas, a sizable edge of northeastern Oklahoma, and contiguous portions of lower Missouri and upper Arkansas.

The geographical boundaries are somewhat fuzzy; so was the formative geology. Apparently the Ozarks began as a towering mountain range, perhaps the aboriginal Himalayas of the West. Eroding eons wore this range down to a farflung plateau which in time covered as much as a third of what is now the United States. As other great mountain ranges were raised to the east and the west, the first Ozarks were buried under an inland sea, then raised again as a high, vaulted mountain range. The wearing down and volcanic blasting up recurred. This third emergence has endured as the present Ozarks "uplift."

In terms of human settlement this uplift lingered for many years as a never-never land. There is good archaeological evidence that the pre-Columbian settlers were comparatively few. Unquestionably they included at least a few Siouan Indians, who presumably, and in the main, inhabited caves in the southern and western fringes of the mountainous plateau. In time, perhaps in the thirteenth and fourteenth centuries, Osages and Quapaws again settled fringe areas; here again the population was apparently small and scattered throughout the region. There is evidence that even before the arrival of white settlers the Indians were ceasing to be year-round residents, using the region principally as hunting grounds. One result is that the Ozarks have no more than an extremely shadowy history of the Indians' culture.

A comparably shadowy background relates to the earlier white colonizers. By the late eighteenth and early nineteenth century the Ozarks were being mentioned occasionally as fur-trapping or "pelting" country. Apparently the trade was slight and carried on principally by Indian or French-Indian itinerants.

Spain's sovereignty hovered from 1762 into 1802, but these four decades left remarkably little enduring evidence of the so-called Spanish hallmark. France's formal dominion of the Ozarks (as part of the Louisiana Territory) endured only thirty-three months and again left only very dim traces, mostly in casual names such as *Bois d'arc, Sainte Phillipi,* or *Petit Jean.* France's Napoleon I showed no discernible interest in constructive colonization; his decree of December, 1802, bluntly prohibited private ownership of lands north of latitude 35.5 degrees, and left the French settlers or other entrepreneurs on their own.

Following the Louisiana Purchase the standoffishness of prospective settlers gradually began to diminish. By 1810, American settlements were at last and at least in the borning. The earliest were usually beside rivers or in a few of the more accessible valleys. By 1810, Revolutionary veterans were being granted homestead lands in the area, in lieu of promised but still uncompensated payment for their military services. The fierce and frenetic War of 1812, in which American troops were paid principally by individual states or, in some instances, by counties or townships, presently served to increase the federal issuance of veterans' land grants in the Ozarks wilds. As of 1812, Springfield, Missouri, was the only clearly recognizable town in the entire area.

Otherwise, Ozarks settlement was achieved mainly by slow and highly individualistic infiltration from older states, particularly mountainous areas of western Pennsylvania, Virginia, Kentucky, and its blossoming daughter, Tennessee. Intermittently, handfuls of German, Austrian, French, Polish, and Irish immigrants moved in, along with earlier settlers from the Ohio Valley. During the 1820's and 1830's limited numbers of Georgians and Alabamians, for the most part hill people, also settled in the Ozarks, particularly on the Arkansas frontier. But the principal settlement remained cautiously gradual and primarily in the northern Ozarks.

Political sovereignty was correspondingly belated. Missouri Territory, which then included virtually all of the Ozarks, was established by an act of Congress of June 4, 1812. Nineteen months later the territorial legislature of Missouri somewhat vaguely established "Arkansa county," which included most of the present state of Arkansas. On March 9, 1817, less than a week after taking his oath as fifth President of the United States, Virginia's James Monroe signed an act of Congress to establish the United States Territory of Arkansas. (Monroe himself may have added the final "s" to the name.)

Official recognition did not change the status of Ozarks remoteness. Settlers came and went, for the most part not easily. Travel by land remained extremely difficult. Missouri remained chronically short of roads; Arkansas was almost completely roadless. River transportation remained severely localized and generally unimpressive. Comparatively little river traffic came nearer the Ozarks than the Mississippi or, after 1820, the Arkansas River. Mail routes were not established until well into the 1830's, in many outlying settlements not before the 1870's. Stagecoach services were comparably delayed; even during the 1850's they were still comparatively scarce.

Throughout the first half of the nineteenth century the Ozarks as a whole remained the lost lands of the New West, a much neglected frontier with a continuing inability to attract or hold its proportionate share of settlers. Although the criterion for settlement was very largely agricultural, in instance after instance the first settlers showed a rather astonishing inability to select favorable farming lands. Again and again first settlers bypassed the more fertile-soiled valleys to homestead or otherwise settle hillsides and mountaintops with appallingly poor soils.

Such settlements either faded completely or "growed up pore." Even by the prevailing status the Ozarks were "sparse country." In 1836, when Arkansas Territory was admitted to statehood, federal census takers estimated somewhat vaguely that the state had 50,000 people; by then Missouri had a "guessed at" census of 200,000. But the total Ozarks population may have been no more than 40,000. The 1840's turned out to be the first decade of visible increase of immigration into the region as a whole. But the incomers' choice was still principally of riding in or coming afoot. The one-time Indian "Southwest Trail," out of St. Louis and skirting only the upper Ozarks, was the only interstate wagon-road. Many of the so-called foot-trail settlers still kept with the Dan'l Boone tradition of moving on as soon as neighbors came within sound of musket shot or sight of chimney smoke.

During the 1850's, while principal areas of the United States East were acquiring railroads, parts of the Ozarks began acquiring their first interstate, in time transcontinental, stagecoach lines, and presently a first bold show of telegraph lines along the "wire roads."

But the remoteness lingered, and its many influences would shape and color the vintages of Ozarks tellin' stories. Persisting illiteracy also had a part in this. For most Ozarks settlers, illiteracy or quasi-literacy came and stayed on, not by invitation or willing acceptance, but by duress of environment and circumstances. Public schools and private schools or "academies" entered the Ozarks principally by way of Missouri. They came scattered and late. One inevitable result was that the settlers were more than ordinarily disposed to telling or recounting stories and to listening to others recount orally because they were seldom able to read or write. Poverty and remoteness were companion contributors. The best available public records indicate that in 1860 twenty-two counties of the Missouri Ozarks had a total of only thirteen public school establishments, while nineteen counties of the Arkansas Ozarks had only three. During 1859, the writer's grandfather, Alfred M. Wilson, who was then the highly itinerant prosecuting attorney for western Arkansas, estimated that hardly more than 20 per cent of that state's people could be called literate. Almost 25 per cent were Negro slaves, and the schooling of slaves was grimly prohibited by state laws which rated it as a felony. Missouri, too, was a slave state, but its Negro population by 1860 was perhaps no more than 10 per cent.

The foregoing is another reminder that slavery had proved itself a double disaster for the persistently agrarian Ozarks economy. Slave ownership was a minority burden. The Parmalle-Reynolds studies made during the 1850's estimated that about 15 per cent of the landowning farmers of the Missouri Ozarks were slaveholders, a proportion then somewhere near the average of the South as a whole. The impeding economic flaw was, of course, that the Ozarks lands were never suited to the basic economy, such as it was, of slave-powered agriculture. Cotton growing and tobacco growing, which had sustained the unholy institution financially, never suited the lands and climate of the region. "Land pore and nigger pore" endured as a perennial lament even of the more prosperous settlers. One rather pertinent recounting of this recurrent and rather outrageous quandary may be found in the distinctly poignant life story of George Washington Carver, who was born and raised a slave in the lower Missouri Ozarks.

◄§ 8 §►

Musing Overture

There is no doubt that the entry of the Negro even as a chattel added memorably to the depths and richness and warmth of Ozarks culture. In turn, the duress emigration of the Negro population was to prove one of the more profound sociological losses of this still engaging and tantalizing region. Far more than any other component of Ozarks populations, the Negro has contributed to its living language, its verve and sensitivity, its durable humor and charm. The slave and his allegedly free descendants had helped the Ozarks to speak, to sing, to dance, to pray, and to know spiritual growth. It followed as night follows day that when so-called emancipation was effected, the Ozarks Negro was presently squeezed out, first southward to seek survival as a cotton sharecropper and in time to seek further as a bottom-of-the-puddle industrial hireling. As a result, Ozarks culture lost grievously in charm and warmth. But neither the Negro nor his "spirit" was wholly lost to the Ozarks tellin' story.

For half a century following the anguish of the Reconstruction, the Ozarks drowsed along as a predominantly rural frontier peopled with yeomen who rather quietly accepted the heritage of thin-pursed self-sufficiency. The slave was no longer on hand for serving as hewer of wood, drawer of water, clearer of new land ("ground") or tender of the young or exhaler of joy. By families and clans a few of his progeny stayed on; but for the most part, with the cramping choice of retreating to the poorest of the poorer farm sites or taking dour refuge in a few of the more permissive towns, there to scrounge along as unskilled laborers or other menials, the Negroes left. At any rate, the creative spirituality of the Negro did not depart totally.

Even so, the embittered, darkly confused Reconstruction years proceeded further to confirm the Ozarks as an agrarian frontier for the diverse descendants of country dwellers from older countries, in great part the British Isles. Not at all surprisingly, the modestly self-provident small landowner or yeoman remained the most definitive resident. Sociologically, it was a procedure of easing back into a hazy, gradually yellowing Indian summer. The likable complacency of the poor yeoman's mood and philosophy, to some degree the living language of England's post-Elizabethan yeomanry, found rather extensive resurrection. So, quite naturally, did the philosophical summations of such particularly revealing earlier-England commentators as Nicholas Breton:

> All the corn we make our bread of groweth on our own demesne ground. The flesh we eat is all, or the most part, of our own breeding. Our garments, also, or much thereof [are] made within our house. Our own malt and water maketh our drink. . . . We have corn in the granery, cheese in the loft, milk in the dairy, cream in the pot, butter in the dish, ale in the tub, beef in the brine, bacon in the [attic], herbs in the garden, and water at our doors. . . What in God's name can we desire to have more?

Ozarkers had all this to tell of orally and, indeed, a great deal more. The taller tales of the Civil War and so-called Reconstruction were recurring verbal resurrections and amplifications. Quite factually the Ozarks had been a rather decisive arena of this bewildering marathon of fierceness, corruption, and mayhem. Significant armies had swept over the Ozarks, and major battles, such as Pea Ridge and Prairie Grove, had been fought there. Border raiders and border warfare had left their violent markings and the too fertile seeds of forthcoming outlaw gangs.

There were more than plenty of war stories to tell and embellish. There were also initially true recountings of localized

clan feuds and the beginnings of colonizing clans. There were substantially factual stories about the burying and finding of money caches. The last mentioned provided material for a long-lived generation of tales related to treasure hunting and occasionally to treasure finding. Certainly the settlers had cause for hiding their savings, dowry, or trading money under hearths or garden walls, in stumps or under turnip bins. The early banks were notoriously flimsy and untrustworthy. With the ominous onset of the Civil War, Ozarkers with even a modicum of money and the sagacity of a chipmunk converted savings to gold and hid it as effectively as they possibly could. Some did not live to recover their money caches; in a great many instances the finders turned out to be keepers. Inevitably the chronicles of treasure finds gained impressive elaborations and were helped along with the restoration of earlier and more folkish yarns relating to "Spaniard gold," the highly fabulous and presumably yet unfound treasure supposedly mined or stolen from conquered Indians by those low-down, hard-hearted, mean, contrary, Con-kiss-ty-doors.

But the Civil War and its aftermath were fantasies of the factual and, in great part, the terrible. The gory fighting, feuding, highwaymanship, looting, and burning did not end or remarkably recede with Lee's surrender. The long-dormant and traditionally anemic law-enforcement agencies, such as they were, found resurrection quite slowly. In some instances the occupation forces were ill disciplined and mendacious, or worse. Along with extreme poverty and spirit-darkening upsets, the Reconstruction era saw the emergence of the Ku Klux Klan and its distinctly Ozarkian counterpart, the Bald Knobbers, a nocturnal thug group which summoned its membership by means of signal fires built on the hilltops.

This historical background of the Ozarks supplied the

factual ingredients of tellin' stories, which throughout the ensuing decades grew, proliferated, and somehow found correlation with the everyday-living stories.

There is very good evidence that the years between 1870 and 1917 turned out to be the most formative and engaging era of Ozarks storytelling. Granting that time did not stand still, for the majority of rural Ozarkers it moved slowly.

The American nation at large was striding and clouting through its longest era of peace. The outrageously contrived five-month Spanish-American War did not reach deeply into the Ozarks. Neither did the grimy and increasing uproar of industrialization. Railroads made penetration and the first mild jags of roadbuilding began. New towns emerged. Hardwood timber industries took pap and nurture, and a few mining centers developed, such as those near Joplin, Missouri. But the more decisive patterns of frayed-shirt and calico-skirt yeomanry endured. The tellin' stories tended to shift from violence, conflict, and passionate quest to the recounting of everyday living and whimsy.

This more than usually sleepy and dream-dusted summertime interval apparently marked the rather extensive beginnings of another somewhat distinctive and home-distilled story quality, the flavoring of Ozarks humor. The somber stories of the great war and its aftermath years almost magically showed leavenings of merriment which were destined to endure for a dozen years or more.

The laughing mood was blooming away like sequestered wildflowers in the early 1920's when this writer began a long-time interlude as a frequently pedestrian country correspondent for various newspapers, most particularly the *St. Louis Post-Dispatch*. My work routine was one of getting into the backwoods and seeing and hearing what was going on. More or less inevitably, the rural crossroads stores became my

more dependable trail markers and the store-porch or counter-side loungers my premier sources of revelation.

My quest involved following a country road or trail to a far-back crossroad where one more or less stumbled into a country store. Almost invariably the store would be garnished with people; not necessarily customers, just country folks come to pass away some time and get on with some whittling and jawing—neither meant to be productive. Some chewed tobacco; a few smoked pipes. They stretched themselves into the general shapes of **X**'s or **Y**'s. They yawned, hummed odd little tunes, smiled a great deal, and, from time to time, laughed aloud.

I recall a fairly typical gathering on the store porch of Weddington Gap, Arkansas. Willie Skeets, Homer Leathers' hired boy, opened the dialogue with his employer. "Homer, how'd hit be was I to ride your hoss home?"

The employer quivered visibly. "Reckon not, Willie. Gotta ride 'im myse'f." Homer's grin expanded. "Mebbe I'd leave you walk aside me——"

The hired boy leered up at his employer. "No siree, bob! Was I to walk alongside you, I'd be havin' to open and shet every gate and fencegap between here and thar."

The afternoon's flow of merriment was opened. Homer Leathers peered down at his lolling hired help. "By the way, Willie, how come you ain't workin'?"

With vast deliberation the youth pushed the remains of a much ventilated straw hat low over his ears and again leered up at his employer. "I *was* workin' . . . Was plowin' corn. But when I come to the end of the row I bounced off and wronched my knee."

A whitening elder recalled how he once came horrifyingly close to falling off the field of grace and wrenching his joints of high principles. "Only I got saved by the Book. Yessir, I had eyesight to read back in them days, and while I was courtin' my wife she asked me what I was readin'. I told her I was lookin' up names for our chilluns. After we'd got wedded, five young'uns come to us—three boys, then a girl, then another boy. So I named 'em Matthew, Mark, Luke, Ann, Jawhn."

The ensuing revelations were locally rooted and unendingly repetitious. Merriment just flowed. It sufficed grandfather, father, and son alike to recall and retell how Uncle Ameriky Hanson got religion at the Schooner Bald revival meeting only to lose it again when his spring buggy bounced off a boulder ledge and broke an axle. Or that Aunt Marthy Pippitt put eggs underneath twenty-six settin' hens, which after three weeks responded by hatching out three pullets and three hundred and ninety-six roosters.

And how the nearsighted gospel singer set out to cross War Eagle River by walking the fallen elm tree that served as a bridge. It was a moon-bright winter's night, but the hymn singer bypassed the real log and approached instead a long black shadow that lay across the narrows. He decided to hunker down and coon across what he took to be the log. So he knelt, put his elbows forward, and painstakingly tumbled head first into the icy water. And the time that hymn-playing fiddler stepped to the preacher's rostrum to strike up "Redeeming Grace, How Sweet Thy Name," only to find that some of them little hellions had larded his fiddle bow so it wouldn't make as much noise as a lightning bug with a sore throat.

Then there were the drolly oblique references. "Over past Loafer's Glory begins the truly dense bresh. Uncle Leander Frost's the only one in all the bend and holler as knows how to read printin'. Come a summertime all the neighbor people chip in and buy the noospaper from Springfield, Missour-ah, so as Pappy Leander can read hit to 'em. One day they was settin' to listen to Pappy readin' where the paper said ever'body had ought to plow the corn deep on account a powerful bad drought was all set to settle in. Back in them parts 'dry spell' is what they call hit when there don't come no rain. Anyway, Mart Miller r'ared his chair back and petted his chin whiskers and chawed his terbacker until finally he said, 'Leander, what's a "drought"?'

"Pappy puzzled for quite a spell and finally he says, 'I ain't a-tall shore, but iffen I ain't too dang wrong, a drought is one of them newfangled varmints that's a cross betwixt a wild hawg and a coon. Anyhow, it's homemade hell on the corn crop!' "

There was a distinctive gentleness in the tone of narration. Consider, for example, the Piety Rally held at the Greasy Creek, Arkansas, schoolhouse. Uncle Zeb Hatfield, who hadn't been at a socializing for a month of Sundays, got nervous and chanced to pour buttermilk instead of cream into his coffee. The old-timer nonchalantly blew at the appalling mess and assured all present that he invariably took buttermilk in his coffee. There wasn't so much as an adolescent snicker.

The same usually held for the confidings of the old-timer who could never get any enjoyment out of reading the dictionary because it changed the subject too golblamed often, or the clodhopper who overwhelmed the schoolteacher's statement that the burning of Mart Miller's barn looked like the work of an incendiary with, "Incindiary, hell, somebody sot it afire!" Or of the onlooking Southern sympathizer at the Battle of Pea Ridge, Arkansas. When a Union cannonball came slithering across the cleared field, good old Luke Kantz just couldn't resist the temptation of giving the Yankee callin' card a contemptuous kick, thereby losing his right foot.

There was no bite or sarcasm in the recounting of how, at the protracted brush arbor meetin' at Avocy crossroads where there had been a long dry spell and crops were virtually ruined, Pastor Porterfield prayed long and appropriately for rain and the recurrence of the parable of feeding the hungry, then began calling on members of the congregation to arise and testify or pray. When Uncle Greene Wilson's turn came he called out, "Lord, go right ahead and pervide fer each accordin' to his needs. Grant to every household a barrel of cured pork, a barrel of molasses, a barrel of flour, a barrel of meal, a barrel of salt, a barrel of pepper—" Corrective pause. "Hell, that's too damned much pepper!"

The foregoing is, or at least seeks to be, an affable reminder that Ozarks humor like all humor is born of surprise and exaggeration. It has been nurtured on whimsy or caprice, and for good measure a strange and engaging sprinkling of satire. Even so, and I sincerely believe it is so, Ozarks tellin' stories are only rarely describable as primarily humorous. The bailiwick of Ozarks humor is principally one of the recounted episode, the expanded quip, the smile-provoking conversation, the passing or repeated whimsy. The speaker's posture, his inflection, the place, mood, and situation of his listener or intimate audience are contributing factors of very real consequence.

More frequently than not Ozarks tellin' stories are chronicles of sadness, resignation, or primitive irony. Sometimes the variants and intermixtures are fringed with a surprising and often delightful satire. There are occasional fruitions of inventive romanticism, or what may be termed elemental story building.

But the Ozarks tellin' story, particularly in its earlier emanation, has been a creation of folkish invention. Although it abounds in conflict and potentials for character development, it is not and it has never been a convenient writing story *per se*. For purposes of type frames and, indeed, of motion picture films or mass broadcasting, the extreme localization, the mood of excessive length and oftentimes confusing details, and the recurring shortage of motivations are more or less chronic detractions. For many years—to the writer's intimate knowledge, at least sixty—most journalistic or more scholarly efforts to interpolate Ozarks tellin' stories have fallen far short of minimal goals of either artistry or craftsmanship.

A cogent long-time Ozarker friend of this writer, "Uncle" Jesse Ford of Pea Ridge (more literally Peavine Ridge, Arkansas), confided, "Seems like there ain't no longer nothin' easy about gettin' a listen to real country tellin' stories. I tell my young people that there is why I do sich a sight of talkin' to myse'f." The back-hill patriarch pointed out that he particularly misses what he terms the old-time tellin' stories: "Now-days if it didn't happen this mornin' or late last night, it ain't no longer a tellin' story."

This, it seems to me, is a particularly cogent entry. Traditionally the Ozarks tellin' story has not been obliged to keep pace with history; certainly it cannot survive the prevailing enslavement by the almost fabulously accelerated stampede of occurring history. Like it or not, we can only appraise the Ozarks tellin' story in the past tense, for as of today, our subject is dying without viable seed.

But death does not belittle life. The Ozarks tellin' story has built monuments more lasting than bronze; it can live and live and live and never die. Speaking as one Ozarker, and a third generation thereof, I most sincerely hope it will.

This book represents one man's quest for restorable tellin' stories of his beloved homeland. I am sorry it is not better than it is, glad and grateful that it is not worse.

THE REEDS GO FORTH

The factual underpinnings of "The Reeds Go Forth" are related to several relevant and reasonably typical facts of Ozarks pioneering. For one such entry, there really were settlers' clans or reasonable facsimiles thereof, including the Reeds and the Dyes. Both began as prolific and rural family groups that were presently joined by in-laws, more distant kin, and miscellaneous frontier neighbors. Both before and after the Civil War, the Reeds and the Dyes settled in the then distant backwoods of a rather large and fairly centrally located Ozarks area, namely Washington County, Arkansas.

Both indulged in somewhere near the prevailing average stint of fighting when most of their men and older boys joined in the various Civil War army or guerrilla forces. Beginning in 1866, the Reeds, then headquartered in or around the present site of Lake Weddington, Arkansas, veered into a bit of feuding and expedient marauding.

Among those whom they disturbed were the Dyes, then principal settlers in the "Little White River Country" between the surviving communities of Greenland and West Fork, Arkansas. The Dyes were law-abiding and respected "folks," for the most part landowning farmers. They had patriarchal leadership without formal title or office. They "stood up for their rights," stood together, and certainly as a group were effective yeomen.

The Reeds also had many good points, but during the anarchistic decade that followed the Civil War, some of them temporarily "went bad." Precisely how bad is largely in the realm of the tellin' stories. Some of the Reeds indulged in group robberies and miscellaneous highwaymanship which violently befell several country stores of the area and deeply disturbed a number of the villages, including the then village-proportioned county seat, Fayetteville, the writer's native town.

The highest crescendo of the marauding materialized in 1871–72. During the latter year, apparently unduly upset by intensified rumors, Fayetteville organized an "armed vigilante company" to defend itself against "them Reed hellions." My father, at eighteen, was a volunteer member and "awk'ard" squad enrollee of that company. The University of Arkansas, then the Arkansas Industrial University (it was not actually a university and not even remotely industrial), was in the initial stages of building. As a land-grant college, however, it had been treated with an "assignment" of otherwise discarded U.S. Army rifles. These were issued to the fifty-four valiant volunteer defenders. After ten days of laborious "drillin'," my father tried out his rifle only to find that the dang thing wouldn't shoot. But fortunately, the Reeds wouldn't raid, either.

The folkish appeal of the Reeds and Dyes feud as a tellin' story which at least grasps at the sleeve of truth is augmented by rootage in confirmable history.

What follows here is this Ozarker's first effort to adapt and, in some part, embroider the versions of this folk story to some degree of coherence. (I was fifteen at the time, the tellin' story was almost four times as old.) While permitting the ensuing to speak for itself, as the printed word persists in doing, it is perhaps not amiss to note that through the years the Ozarkian concept of clan has remained ephemeral and conversational. Its relevance, so far as it has any, has tended to relate to far rural communities or backwoods neighborhoods which, from time to time, have joined together in attempts to stand against forces that would destroy them. That held for the respective clans of the sometimes aggressive Reeds and the predominantly peaceful Dyes.

THEY had walked far that day, along dimming country roads and disappearing trails, through woods and fields still winter gray and brown. But the winter was ending. In the deeper valleys the invaders came on carpets of brave new grass. There the redbuds were coming into blossom; there red oak buds were swelling, and the new poplar leaves were nearing the size of mouse's ears.

On the higher hillsides the forest shadows were still thin and chill, and the tramping was slippery and otherwise trying. Even so, the Reeds pushed on, grimly determined to prove to themselves and all others that they really were a war party with a manly and warlike mission; they were on their way to meet the Dyes and smite them down. And it was now or never; without just or sensible cause the Dyes were coming up while the Reeds were going down. Sometimes life is like that, even though it hadn't ought to be.

The Reeds trudged along in single file, for the most part grimly silent. All but two of their nineteen members had fought and raided before as Confederate guerrillas; only the eldest and the youngest of their force were without experience as armed invaders. The two neophytes were of ages rather ridiculously far apart. Old Hal Reed, long a great-grandfather, admitted to being eighty-three; it was expert agreement that the old-timer was actually a good many years older than he chose to tell. The youngest of the war party, one of the younger of old Hal's great-grandsons, was only sixteen. By common agreement the Reeds did not favor taking doddering old men or fuzzy-faced boys on war parties. But no Reed ever told old Hal what he couldn't do, since he was as set in his ways as a kingpin wildcat and the closest thing they had to a clan leader. And they had brought along young Abel for good cause—to serve as scout or point. Quite aside from being poet-faced and disgustingly handsome, that Abel knew the back hills better than any one of his elders; better, for that matter, than all of them together. For good measure, the youngster was sharp-eyed and fleet-footed and sharp like a trailing timberwolf. That Abel was, therefore, the surest safeguard against ambush or traps, at which the Dyes excelled, and he could lead a way out of enemy country as well as into it, a competence that could well be a lifesaver. And the Dyes could get tough; fact was, they'd never turned tender.

Near the first limestone rim of Weddington Mountain, Abel tarried. He found himself enjoying the cautious gentleness of the young springtime. Here and there along the very dim trail he noted tassels of brown-red earth newly lifted by earthworms—testimony that the trail had not been used for many days. But the youngster gave particular heed to the bird life nearby. He saw a troupe of cardinals at play in the early leafing haw bushes, watched a field lark flit down as if to a newly established nesting place. There was feathered evidence that the new springtime was well on its way. He heard a raincrow call from the top of an oak tree still brown from unshed leaves.

Rain. Abel was piecing together a succession of rain signs. The night before there had been a whitish circle around the moon and inside that circle a single star. That was a sky message foretelling rain within twenty-four hours. And the sky tells only truth; the moon and stars are eternal lamps hung out to show the signs and seasons. Like as not the rain crow had read the sign. But people—slow, stupid, hating, pretending to be warriors . . . . He heard the rain crow again and, from his place of vantage, watched the heavy-gaited line of Reeds wagging into the open valley directly ahead. Somewhat pensively, Abel kicked away a swath of dead leaves. In doing so, he uncovered a wild violet, half-open. Without trying to interpret, he picked his way around an encircling boulder and knelt, ear close to the ground. From the mountains far to the south he was certain that he heard a sound, as if of far-off piping, a strange, thin melody, played through reeds. He had heard it before in the Sulphur Mountain country. But he did not surely know its source.

But now from his left front he heard what was no doubt meant to be a thrush call. It came again, stolid and piercing, as if whistled through chapped lips. Abel laughed. The Reeds would use a thrush song as their very special clan call, but they had never learned to make it sound convincingly real. That had been going on as long as he could remember. And so, mostly in derision, the Reeds had been given the name of "thrush people." At any rate, Abel knew that he was being summoned.

He ambled up the next hillside to avoid the seepy morass through which the trail led, then followed a rock-littered ravine down the far side of the hill. Within a very few minutes he found himself among his elders, who could hardly have picked a more conspicuous place for holding a parley. Squire John Reed began delivering the reprimand, but Squire Henry, the toothless, took over:

"Young sprout, I'm axin' you what's the idee of hangin' back like a bull calf on t'other end of a leadin' rope? If you was gettin' what you got rightfully comin' to you, it'd be a good thrashin'. This ain't no time fer pickin' daisies. This what we're doin' is war, onderstand!"

There was glowering agreement as his uncle Gren Reed took over. "You been sayin' how you knowed this country through here. Now let's hear where we're gettin' to. Onderstand, we want to keep straight. And, let me tell you, if we get trapped from behind 'cause 'o' your dallyin', this time tomorry your hide won't hold daylight. Where you figger we're at as of right now?"

"Well, I figger," Abel answered, chewing nonchalantly at a sassafras twig, "that we're startin' to head for the second slope of Sulphur Mountain and that in another good two hours we'll be to the head of Dye's Valley."

He noted that some of his kin seemed visibly disturbed by the mention of "Dye." Gren Reed peered across the brush-grown valley toward the more massive mountain beyond. Wisps of cloud drifted below him.

Abel considered reminding the self-commissioned captain that he and his followers were halted in easy view of any watcher. He was quite confident that the Dyes had their look-outs ready placed. But he reported dutifully: "I'd call it three more hours of trampin' and two more of fair daylight. . . ."

He was mildly surprised when his uncle agreed. "That's fair clost to what I figger."

"Two hours would about get us to the brown saplin' timber," Abel suggested.

"Well, gem'men, the trick is, as I figger it, to bivouac tonight in a likely tater-knob holler an' cut down the head of the valley at early dawn."

"Not camp in the hollow!" Abel gasped. "It'll come rain tonight."

At that point, Squire Jason Reed cut in, "How in thundera-tion do *you* know, young'un? Talk like you was Jupiter Pluvius's pup or somethin'."

The captain grinned, as if in boredom. "Run along, boy! I can't see a rain cloud nowhere, and we won't borry trouble."

"The sun went down red last night," observed a gruff-voiced hillman. There was general agreement.

Gren Reed closed the discussion. "Climb on yer hind legs

and get movin'! Hit's a fur piece yet today. An' tomorry this time they'll be Dyes layin' fer buzzard bait all the way from here to yander."

Abel turned back to his post, now heavy-heartedly aware that he was showing the way to kill, all without the makings or grounds for hating or fighting. Why should the Dyes be warred on? Abel had heard the stock answers: The Dyes were a great passel of scoundrel rich folks who, back in Civil War times, had taken over the big, rich horseshoe valley at the far end of Sulphur Mountain. There they were thriving by robbing and pillaging and terrifying the honest hill people, or so said the Reeds.

But Abel had long since ceased to believe all his people said. He had his own reasons to believe that the Dyes and Reeds had put together their respective clans in similar fashion. The real difference was that the Dyes had waxed strong in their valley, which they had been able to defend against all who would invade it. The Reeds, by contrast, had not planned or taken or held together anywhere near so successfully. During the war years, when raider bands and other marauders had gained a kind of asylum as soldiers without uniforms or certain cause, the Reeds had been beaten back from Dye company. They now feared the vengeance while coveting the goods of a stronger and richer clan.

Abel had heard tall yarns about the Dyes, that all were near-giants, deadly with firearms, completely fearless. He did not surely believe or disbelieve all he had heard. More particularly, he did not understand why the Reeds should hate the Dyes and make war against them. Abel had seen the Dyes once; had watched a party of them ride through Red Star, the village of the Reeds, when he was very young. He could hear again the ring of their horses' hoofs on the flat-rock paving. He recalled that they were big men, but to a toddling child, most grownups and all horsemen look big. He remembered how one party of riders had dismounted in front of Skelt's saloon and called for liquor. When Skelt Reed had fetched it, they drank and asked that he pay himself. They wondered if he would mind feeding and watering their horses? This no sooner suggested than done, one of the Dyes had stepped over to Epperly's general store and asked for a dollar's worth of flannel suitable for cleaning muskets. The storekeeper measured out half a bolt and forgot to accept the offered dollar. Then the Dyes rode once around the town and headed southwest in the general direction of Sulphur Mountain. The gunbearers of the settlement had kept strangely out of sight. Not a single Reed protested in person.

Some hours after the riders had left, another stranger rode up from the south, a rather oldish man, quiet, tall, and somewhat stooped. He went first to the saloon and asked that he might be let pay for the free servings; and he paid with round, clanking, silver dollars. Next, he stepped across to Epperly's store, listened to the keeper's account of having been robbed of flannel, then paid the sum, leaving a dollar extra for the clerk.

Up to that point all went well. But then Gren Reed, who had been conspicuous only for his absence, came out from the back spaces of his Uncle Skelt's saloon, stepped in front of the elderly stranger, grabbed his horse's bridle rein and shouted in a mighty voice, "I'll lay my right arm to it, here's old Ephram Dye!"

The patriarch did not deny it. Then, other of the Reeds began to pour forth from back places with heated argument and dark mutterings.

Still, old Eph Dye stood his ground, explaining that he had

come to make good any ill behavior of his young kinsmen or their companions; also that he came alone and unarmed, and he had reckoned to come and go in peace.

The Reeds reckoned differently. Some suggested holding the old fellow as a hostage; others said that he had best be hanged on general principles. To discourage longer parley, Gren Reed laid strong hands on the old man, pulled him from his saddle, called for a strap, bound his wrists behind his back, and, having searched him to no avail, looked toward his horse.

Now the veteran Dye carried plump saddlebags, each marked with a luck sign, the imprint of a horseshoe. And the saddlebag yielded rich booty! One of them was heavy with money—some six hundred dollars in silver and greenbacks. The other bag was crammed with personal belongings of no great value but well worth taking.

Having relieved him of his possessions, young Gren strolled over to a spot where the youngsters had been pitching horseshoes, selected a likely shoe, gathered up a handful of kindling wood, built a fire with it, and laid the horseshoe on the fire.

"Now, men, was you askin' me, I'd say, put a mark on him as will help him to recollect about stayin' to home and mindin' his own clearin's."

There was assent. Young Gren let the horseshoe heat to a cherry red, picked it up with a pair of firm-handled tongs—fetched from the store—and laid an arc of the shoe, sizzling hot, firmly against old Eph Dye's cheek.

There was an odor of scorching flesh. A shudder of pain went through the old man's body, but not a sound came from his lips. And there was a quarter of the oval of the horseshoe burned deep into his flesh, a great scar, livid and terrible.

The experiment finished, the Reeds lifted the old fellow to his saddle, facing him toward his horse's tail, tied the bridle reins beneath his armpits, and, giving his horse a cut across the rump with a quirt, headed him in the general direction of Sulphur Mountain. Two of the young Reeds followed to see more of the fun. Less than an hour later their horses trotted back to Red Star, riderless. The Reeds were fewer by two.

Owls were noisy that night, and every Reed capable of walking beneath the weight of a musket helped patrol the village of Red Star. No violence came of it, however, and for nearly ten years the clans had kept close, each to its own.

But now the Reeds were gone forth, to surprise and have out a battle to a finish. For every year the Dyes were increasing in numbers and strength, while the Reeds were coming to be always poorer and fewer as more and more of their young men slipped off to the plains country to the ways of the wind. Gren Reed had succeeded as leader, and he chose to go forth for conquest now, while blood was still thick and strong with winter.

Abel stood alone in the late sunlight. On the hillsides above him were swaying acres of new grass; beneath him were rolling fields and distant stretches of sky. On the horizon to the northwest lay a rim of slate-gray clouds. He had expected as much—what with the rain crow and all.

He heard again the far faint melody of pipes as if from some high hill pasture. For a moment he pondered, then arose and climbed, following the sound. Presently he came upon a path which seemed strange to him, for paths usually follow the valleys. But this one circled among mighty oak trees, higher and higher up the mountainside. He heard the pipes again, more clearly. The path cut in sharply, and Abel climbed a mighty stairway of outcropping granite. He came out upon a level hilltop.

There the piping was close at hand. Staying close to the fringe of underbrush, Abel looked out. A scattering of sheep grazed near him, raised their heads, sniffed curiously, and passed on. A young lamb sprang up suddenly, as if wakened from a dream too beautiful to be longer endured. Then Abel looked down on a great sweep of pastureland and saw a young woman fingering a set of pipes—a curious instrument. Long pipes hung from her shoulder. With her right hand she played a melody on a thin, dark fife, pressing the while a bag covered with a green and black plaid. The wind played through her dark brown hair, and beyond her appeared the main body of the flock, docile and sleepy, with fleece golden in the slanting sunlight.

Abel recalled that he had heard of shepherd people far back in the hills who still played bagpipes. For sound carries far in the great quiet pastures, and the music soothes the sheep.

The beauty of the scene came upon Abel in a glorious sweep—flocks and pasture and shepherd girl. She seemed to him like a beautiful painting against a background of open sky, her garments held close to her body, her breasts high. About her shoulders she wore a spangled shawl.

Abel halted. When she turned he would surely be found out, but he did not want to slip back into hiding. At sight of him, the music stopped and the pipes squawked like a molested covey of mudhens. In her confusion, the girl let the bagpipes slip to the ground.

Fighting through his timidity, Abel stooped, picked up the pipes and held them out to her.

Her color deepened. She turned, made as if to leave, then deciding otherwise, turned toward Abel half-smiling, and took the instrument. When she laughed, her teeth showed like pearls.

"Might I ask who you be?" she said.

"My name is Abel, Abel Reed."

"Abel Reed? What in the world are you doing here?"

"I—I came because they told me to. You see, I——"

The silence became chilling. Abel stumbled on. "I'm sorry if—if it don't please you. But I was told, you know, and we have to do as we're told——"

She looked long at him. About her lips, now pressed firmly together, he sensed the shadow of a smile. Then she spoke slowly, "Were I to do what *I* was told to, I would just blow a puff like this"—but she didn't—"and then, before long, you just wouldn't be."

The truth came to his bewildered senses. What a blundering dunce he had been—he, a "point," up in the enemy's country, to let a silly girl make mock of him! Of course, he knew *now*. She was a Dye.

"But I won't do what I'm told, you see." She spoke solemnly, like a child burdened with a noble secret.

Abel looked long at her. "Then mayn't we pass as friends?"

She regarded him for a moment, then, feeling his tremendous seriousness, she laughed. To Abel the universe listened entranced.

"I suppose we may as well."

She laid aside the pipes and found a seat in the caressing wild grass. Abel sat at a worshipful distance. Then, without foreplanning, he began to talk. In the course of an hour Abel told her more about himself than he had ever put into words before. When the sun was low, he helped her round up the sheep, and then they walked together, hand clasped in hand.

Gren Reed thought it well to cheer his men a bit that night in order that they might wake more fight-brittle the next morning. This was soldiery. So he sang and jigged in the firelight, a self-described fighting man, grotesque in his childishness. Old Hal Reed succeeded in repressing his annoyance. After nightfall, a camp song carries far among the quiet hills;

this he knew. But he made no protest, for the years had taught him caution.

The campfire popped and spluttered as it bit into the dead oak, and showers of sparks arose. Old Hal puffed at his pipe. Gren was everlastingly overdoing. The fire was useless—wastefully big for so warm a night—especially considering that there were no victuals to be cooked except pack bacon. What of the fire didn't go for warmth would surely go for show. Only fools build big campfires. Then there was the business of pitching camp in a cupped hollow on a night when a storm was brewing.

Gren Reed was annoyed by the clan's lifelessness. "Ain't no harm in cuttin' a few pigeon's wings," he repeated. "We be a fur piece from Dye's Holler, and anyhow, this time tomorry night, they won't be no Dyes."

The words sounded empty. The back-hill warriors squatted about the fire in somber silence. Firelight played upon the tall wigwam of their stacked muskets. The moon climbed above a patch of timber. A white circle surrounded it, but inside that circle there was not a single star. A chorus of tree frogs responded to a damp gust of night wind. In disgust, Gren abandoned his attempts at entertainment. One after another the hillmen shouldered their packs and went forth to locate sleeping places on the slope of the valley.

Finally, the leader of today and the leader of yesterday sat alone, smoking in silence. The fire died down.

"They's rain in the wind," old Hal observed.

"Well, croak, ye damned old tree frog!"

Gren, plainly nettled, went about making preparations for the night. Having selected a spot of convenient slope, he clawed out a depression for his hips, threw down his pack blanket, squeezed his felt hat into a wad and laid it for a pillow, then buttoned his coat tight, and lay down, his feet toward the patch of embers where the fire had been.

"Goin' to bed?" he inquired of his companion.

"No, boy, I reckon not. If I was to, I'd jest have to get right back up again. Hit's goin' to rain tonight—shore's I'm settin' here an' you're layin' there. When it commences, they ought to be somebody handy to wake them lads up. 'Cause, take a hard show'r, these here cup hollers fill full o' water 'fore a man could twicet say 'scat.' 'Sides, in a fightin' party, they ought to be somebody keepin' watch."

"Suit yourself."

There was silence. The old man leaned forward, cupped a hand to his right ear and listened. He heard what he had rather expected to hear—the shivering, distant, all too human wail of a screech owl. To the northwest the horizon lightened, and the old hillman felt a drop of rain on his forehead. The night wind climbed higher.

Gren Reed woke to see a first-class demonstration of pandemonium, bright blue spangles of lightning, a crashing cannonade of thunder, a roaring scramble of storm winds, then a battering downpour of cold rain. A hand was at his throat, a cold hand, hard as steel. It was old Hal, shaking the very breath out of him. Gren was on his feet in an instant, fully awake. He shucked off his coat and threw it over the top of the musket stack. He cupped his hands to his mouth and shouted for all he was worth. He splashed through water, already boot-top deep in the lower bed of the hollow, and kicked at the prostrate forms of his followers. "Up and out, ever'body, quick! Grab guns! Sling pack! Git out!" Punctuating his commands with more oaths and kicks, he made the rounds of the bivouac, and presently the sleepers came straggling out of the water trap, drenched to the skin.

Gren took the lead again as the column of invaders floundered up the trail. And so the hillmen scrambled higher, fighting for footing, holding to the rock-strewn path for dear life while sheets of icy water swept down the mountain upon them. Presently old Hal suggested a halt.

"Strikes me we're gettin' lower ag'in. Groun' water shore is worser. I figger we done passed the dee-vide."

But the long hour of plodding and sousing had not weakened Gren Reed's determination, nor had it strengthened his respect for the counsel of his senior. Was he to stand there and take up rain all the balance of the night? He was not! He was going to lead on now until shelter could be found. Then they would dry themselves, look to the muskets and ammunition. Close up to the Dye country, they would be fit for the morning's labor; they could get quickly into action. There would surely be a house or barn somewhere. For years there had been word of lumbermen at work up on Sulphur Mountain.

There were bickering and mutterings, to be sure, but where Gren Reed led, his troopers followed. The footing was level for a way; then came a sharp descent. Gren led down. The invaders followed.

To the south, another aurora of lightning burned threateningly. In the half-light from it, now a hundred paces before them, were the welcome outlines of a long loghouse, blunt-ended and apparently commodious. And down from it there was a shadowy suggestion of more buildings—a logging camp, perhaps, or possibly a mill settlement—at any rate, shelter. The invaders made for it.

Gren Reed stepped heavily on the porch and, having located the latchstring, flung open the door, omitting the formality of knocking.

Inside was darkness, unbroken save for a faint glimmer of light from a half-buried fire. Gren Reed tried to strike a match, but finding his matches soaked to a paste, he pounded upon the door frame with a heavy fist. Scarcely had his knuckles touched wood when the darkness gave forth words, words of drawling hospitality, "Come in, gentlemen! Come in!"

The voice seemed tired and old and none too steady. Then there was a faltering step, a long swish of a match head rubbing against flat board, followed by a flicker of light as the match was set to the tip of a candle.

"Come in, gentlemen! I'll stir the fire."

"We'd be obliged if ye would." Taken aback at the appearance of ready hospitality, Gren Reed pulled off his hat, doused it against his knee, and relayed the invitation to his followers.

"An' I hope we don't bother ye, what with all this water," he added.

"Oh, no bother about the water. Fire soon dries water." This time the voice was easier.

"That's a-talkin', friend! That's a-talkin'!"

Until now the speaker had been cupping the candle flame, but now he took his hand away and they saw a stooped, old man in a long grizzly cape. He was fully dressed. The candlelight reddened his thin hand, but of his face they could see only the shadowed outline.

The old man set the candle in a pewter holder on the mantelpiece. He then stooped before the fireplace, his face away from the clan, stirred from the ashes a round of pink embers, dropped upon them a bagful of fagots, and, reaching far back into a jet-black corner, began laying on stick after stick of firewood. In no time at all red flames took hold and the fire was made. The host, keeping well back among the shadows, turned and beckoned the strangers to accept the hospitality of the hearth.

This they did readily. Water-soaked packs were loosened, and butts of heavy muskets clanked to the floor.

"You are armed?" the old man asked, with rising apprehension.

"We was carryin' a few weapons, yes," Gren Reed admitted tolerantly, edging closer to the hearth.

"I would rather, I mean to say, would you mind leaving the firearms outside?" The tone was uneasy and the speaker seemed pressed upon by dread. "I'm getting old and rickety, and I can't help being opposed to firearms." Gren was amusedly complaisant.

"Stack muskets ag'in the dry side the porch," he commanded. "No, wait! First, we'd best dry 'em off a bit."

The old man appeared relieved.

"You were caught in the storm?" he inquired.

"Friend, we shore was!"

"None of your party was lost by the way, I trust?"

"No."

The fire was rising, and the invaders sprawled in a half-circle about the hearth, wiping the barrels and muzzles of their guns, trying sights and triggers, their wet shoes steaming, and their bodies basking in the welcoming warmth. As if by afterthought, Gren Reed was counting his followers. As he turned to repeat the count, he had a distinct sensation of being watched keenly from behind. But when he looked over his shoulder, he saw that his host was well back in the shadows, his face toward the empty end of the great room.

"Seventeen *due* to be; all I get sight of now is fifteen. Well, there's the fool boy somewhere outside, but that's no great matter. Now let's see, who else? Grandpa Hal, he's not here neither."

Gren Reed would have sworn that he heard someone laugh—a dry old laugh, like the swish of dead leaves. But his host's face was still turned away, and the fire burned lustily.

"Pore old Hal! Dropped out, I reckon! Old laigs is weak. Well——" but Gren preferred to dismiss the subject, and obviously no one objected.

"Gentlemen, there's wood a-plenty for the night, and in the loft above the hallway outside you'll find burlap for bedding."

"Well, friend, we're shore obliged to ye," was Gren's reply.

"But if it isn't too much to ask, would you mind stacking your firearms outside, now that they're dry?" the thin old voice entreated.

"I reckon not, mister. Lee, take up the muskets an' stack 'em in the dry outside."

Strange tracery of shadows played upon the plastered wall. Now above the mantelpiece was a glimpse of a shadowed profile, a rather terrible profile, as of a wrinkled old face with jagged teeth. And all in a minute, Gren changed his order.

"Wait! Not outside! Set 'em inside, there ag'in the door." It was done, and the burlap was brought.

"Prejudice, no doubt, about the guns, gentlemen. Whim of an old man."

"Well, I reckon we all get to be old men, if we live long enough," said Gren.

"Yes, yes. True! That is, if we are accorded the good grace of being let live—a grace undeserved by many."

"You said it ag'in, pardner."

The bedding was spread, and the invaders were making ready for a second sleep. More wood was piled on the fire; shoes were aligned in a half-circle about it to dry.

"But firearms—I dread firearms," the old man persisted.

The Reeds' host ambled over toward the far wall and sank down in a low, straight-backed chair. His head bent forward until his chin touched his chest. His thin old hands were buried deep in his cape pockets.

Most of the invaders slept, but Gren lay in drowsy meditation. Queer old codger, to choose to sleep sitting up! But old men are strange-like and sometimes monstrous clever. Old Hal, now . . . But old men are queerish creatures. . . . Gren Reed slept fitfully. Then he started, as if from a bad dream. A screech owl? Sure, only a crazy screech owl, and surely all was well. The men slept, and there was the old codger, sitting motionless as a sphinx. Gren dozed again.

A cock crew, and Gren woke, wide-eyed. The room was filled with swinging light. And there in front of him, above the mantelpiece, was the outline of a lean, laughing face.

With a great oath partly of terror, Gren sprang to his feet.

The old man was standing before him. In one hand he held a lantern, in the other a heavy pistol, leveled at the leader's throat. There came a medley of voices from outside. Gren's glance went toward the doorway.

But there, instead of guns, were men. Three men stood at the door: dark, big men, heavily armed. Behind them were vague shapes of half a dozen more.

And now the invaders were waking, blinking, cringing, pitiful in their defenselessness. The far end of the room, too, was lined with armed men, all waiting, with death at their fingertips. So these were the Dyes! The Reeds had stumbled into their trap—caught like so many stupid rabbits. The Dyes had them, without so much as a swing of the fist.

"Listen to me!" The old man spoke, not in an uncertain drawl this time, but with the sharp precision of one accustomed to command. He lifted the lantern slowly until its light fell upon his face. Slowly he turned his head. There, in full view, was the arc of the horseshoe, branded deep into his left cheek. It was old Dye.

"Gren Reed, back in our young days, as all remember, you and your associates celebrated my appearance at Red Star with this gift-mark. I am not a man of hate and vengeance. But I still wear the mark of your questioning. In my time you and your men will know my final answer."

One of the Dyes came forward. "Two are missing, sir. Our watch yesterday reported seventeen in the party, including the boy who was trailing alongside."

"Yes, yes, and the other's the old leader. We seem to be getting careless. Can we afford that?"

"No sir, we can't," the younger Dye replied solemnly.

But the old man laughed, this time more like the cackle of a blue jay. "At least, nephew, you played your hand tolerably well. It was I who slipped. Well, to speak truthfully, I'd hardly expected to trap the old bird. And the young one we didn't want especially. Well, we'll take what the storm brought in and be satisfied."

The leader of the Dyes straightened. "Fall them in! March them to the big stable and lock them up. I'll decide their sentences in my own way and time. All Dyes are dismissed. Duty well done deserves good rest. Good night to all!"

The Dyes were crowding to search the prisoners and place them in line. Then they marched their captives to the village road outside and down a brush-hedged lane to a great log stable. A Dye swung open the door and, when the Reeds were counted in, he closed the door and fastened a heavy iron lock. "You've still got the shank of a night to live by!" Clearly the Dyes' words were not meant to be consoling.

Down the lane another Dye began whistling a snatch of song—a carrying tune, lighthearted and easy-flowing, not unlike tunes that may have rung through other hills of other countries during centuries gone by. A salute of blue smoke rose from a flatrock chimney, telling that dawn was very near.

The Reeds, meanwhile, grimly silent, waited what the morning and the expected vengeance of a scarred old man would bring them. After many long minutes, they heard again the oddly pleasant marching song. But this time the voice was that of a girl.

There was another interval of silence. A twig snapped. Then came distinguishable sounds of footsteps—at least two sets of them. Around the bend of the lane appeared two flapping figures in dragging gray capes with sleeves incongruously long, and caps pulled low and collars turned high to hide the wearers' faces.

The newcomers stopped outside, conversing in whispers. Moments later, the Reeds heard the scraping of a key, and for a second time the heavy lock clicked. There was a determined tugging from without. Then the door swung wide.

One of the cape wearers spoke in a lowered voice that most of the Reeds recognized as young Abel's. "Move out fast. Follow the flood gully up the bend to the left. It leads out to a shelf land. Take the left-hand trail from there. Sight for Weddington Gap. . . . Now, move lively!"

Another trap? Maybe. But death was the alternative. By making the dash, they might at least have the chance to raise a hand in self-defense. So the Reed invaders filed out of the door and ran forth like sheep newly freed from a slaughterhouse. Hurriedly and crowding one another, they rushed into the steep mow of the flood gully. When they reached the open shelf land, they found themselves free men, and before them was the morning star to guide by.

Meanwhile, the two figures in overlength capes waited for

a time near the stable door. Then whispering intently they disappeared down a lane still crowded with shadows.

A shot rang out from the lower end of the valley—and another. Then followed a great scampering of feet. Moments later, the oldest Dye was roused by a great banging at his door. He barely had time to climb out of bed when he found himself facing his tall grandson who was holding before him—a mighty hand grasping an arm of each—a brown-haired girl and a serious, blue-eyed boy. The pair still wore disheveled and mud-splashed sentry capes.

"Our prisoners are loose and gone!" the younger Dye shouted. He added less loudly but no less grimly, "and this pair here turned them loose! This boy, the young pip of a Reed we couldn't locate last night." He shoved the maiden forward with formidable emphasis—"And this young lady— my own daughter! She was still carrying the key when we caught her. When I got home, I found her missing from her room. So I went searching. But not soon enough . . ."

By now half a dozen Dyes had crowded into the room and others were peering in the doorway. The old Dye called out for silence. He then addressed his grandson. "I'm not telling you what to do, young man."

"I know exactly what to do, sir." The tall man began un- buckling his heavy belt. "With your permission, sir—I'll begin with this young lady, here. And when I'm done, I'll take on her young playmate, with your permission——"

"I can't seem to recall giving permission . . ." But the old man could not finish. The daughter of a Dye wrenched herself free and stood before the patriarch, her body taut in defiance.

"Go ahead and beat me!" she invited. "But don't dare touch *him*! The fault isn't his. When his people ran into your trap, I let them out—and he did only what I told him to.

"And I'm glad I *did* turn the Reeds loose," she continued heatedly. "For we were right, and you were wrong. And we're not afraid—not afraid."

The lines of the old Dye's face wrinkled in a confusing mingling of smiles and frowns. "Stand up before me, you young clowns! Now—to begin with *you*, young lady, remember that for a shepherd girl to corral her sheep and then spend the night wandering around in a spring freshet brings no comfort either to her parents or to her doddering old ancestor! And after going through the tricks of trapping a clump of stupid clodhoppers capable of learning a lesson only from the one master they can respect—fear—and then having one's great-granddaughter come dragging in scarce an hour before dawn and bringing with her a young male that happens to be one with our enemy . . . ."

The old man paused for breath. "And then the two of you coming to my quarters, disturbing an old man's rest, making more noise than a span of wild colts getting into my hallway, snitching my keys, and snatching up a couple of sentry capes which, heaven knows, on you are misfits by a foot in every direction——"

With one inclusive gesture, old Dye clasped the boy and girl in his arms, his face beaming.

"But it *takes* young clowns now and then to put us old clowns straight. I say, in little ways you two were wrong; in bigger ways you were right. At least you two served us all as peacemakers. Peace is a precious stuff, and all of us at least can hope those Reeds by now have a bellyful of breaking it. Anyway, I'm not expecting them back. That's my speech for today, and for many days to come."

The old man stepped back to his bedside. "Are there any questions—simple questions, that is, that a stupid old man could help answer?"

The old leader's grandson, respectfully determined, stepped before him. "I've got questions, sir. After we'd taken over those rapscallions, why did you have them put into that old stable with only a spiked lock? And that done, why did you call in the whole watch at one time, leaving it so that most any scamp or pair of scamps could turn the prisoners loose?"

"Those are good questions! Well put, and worthy of an answer. Let me see, how old are you, boy?"

"Thirty-eight, sir."

"Thirty-eight, is it? And I am eighty-eight. That puts me an even half a century ahead of you. But getting back to your questions: what I recommend is, that you wait till you're my age, and then try answering them yourself."

SATYR IN ARKANSAS

The story that follows may not be meticulously truthful, but it is for freely believing or disbelieving, trusting or distrusting, precisely as one pleases. Personally, I don't believe a damned word of it, yet I trust it utterly and regard it as timeless.

So far as I know for sure, the story line is wholly fabricated. Furthermore, the characters are mostly fictitious, and I have never actually heard such a yarn told—except in bits or snatches which have been included but without truthful correlation with the principal body of the story.

I have never seen a satyr in Arkansas or anywhere else, but I have seen and known comical hypocrites, in the Ozarks and out. The real quest here is to present the mood and spirit, so far as attainable, in the living speech of real Ozarkers whom I have known and in whom I have found delight. "I" am not important; the perceptive satire, its primitive depths and pertinence are all that really count. They are of the humble magnificence of the backwoods mind, spirit, and hard-to-beat-down integrity of Ozarks culture.

TRADE at Lyin' Johnny Wells's store directly past Nellie's Apron, Arkansas, was about as usual. There wasn't any. So much so that Lyin' Johnny had gone gar fishing, leaving his wife's cousin, Leander Seamster, to take care.

While I probed and pondered the combination of the lock on the cookie bin, Cousin Leander continued to pay his regards to the gallon jug that Lyin' Johnny usually left back of the hat peg directly beyond where the rolled oats and canned peaches came together. After four or maybe five lift-ups, Leander poured out a dipperful for later on and set the empty jug next the store cat, which was sleeping in the snap beans beside the broom basket. That finished, he glanced down at me somewhat diagonally and stated that the next to the last would-be cookie moocher hadn't cracked the combination either, but at least my predecessor had arisen as part and parcel of a true, living parable, same being a sight more than Lyin' Johnny's cousin-in-law felt disposed to expect of me.

To clear the reference, Cousin Leander explained that he was speaking directly of Deacon Cato Fietz, who practically exactly a week before, while squatting beside the same cookie bin and fritzing with the same lock had been inspired and transformed by a Great Moral Awakening.

The last named was not directly connected with the rightfulness of trying to filch ginger snaps and fig newtons but with the wrongfulness of permitting young people of today to get so wicked many moth holes of sin gnawed into the fibers of their characters.

When Kink Marcus and Tola Ames chimed in their amens, Deacon Fietz gets so touched that he stood up and forthrightly stated that it was high time for right-principled citizens to begin putting their feet square down; otherwise rightfulness won't never triumph.

At just that point, Cato Fietz chanced to remember that a crowd of young whippersnappers in Panther Scald deestrict, some seven miles the far side of Nastyville, were set to have a dancing caper at the meetin' house that very night, same being Saturday, and most likely the antics would be endin' with one of those spirit-degrading swimming parties in Catfish Creek. Naturally, the Deacon figured that the most virtuous and patriotic thing any passel of high-minded, virtue-loving citizens like, for example, Cato Fietz, Kink Marcus, and Tola Ames could contribute would be to sneak out and break up the caper, thereby taking the weapon of sin from the unsteady and unrealizing hands of the young while there was still time.

Kink and Marcus said they felt the same way, deeply and throughout. By then others were joining the expression of righteous sentiments. But when starting time came, Lafe Stubblefield recollected that night air worsened his asthmy and Homer Leathers recollected he had to get back to his bloated cow, but Homer just chanced to have out in his pick-up truck the most of a half-gallon of homemade corn licker that maybe wasn't quite tasty enough to sell but plenty good enough to drink. Deacon Cato, allowing he never drank licker except while alone or with somebody, sampled the rotgut and passed the jug to Kink, who did likewise and responded like he had maybe swallowed a live tree frog. He passed along the uplifter of spirits to Tola Ames, who yelled like he was calling out the Nastyville fire department. But all three were finding a sight of uplift for the spirits.

So, came sundown and another emptied jug, Cato and Kink and Tola bought a store counter supper of canned salmon and soda crackers on credit and girded for the call of duty uptrail at or near the Panther Scald Meeting House. After maybe three miles as the crow flies and seven as the trail turns and maybe nine or ten as the three uplifters staggered, Tola recommends a short detour to possibly pick up another half-gallon that Uncle Abe Henstuffer had stashed under a rotten oak stump, and they figured to take and use now and pay for later—perhaps.

After considerable looking, the uplifters located the stump with the licker jugs inside and under, but because even one jug was too heavy for a man to carry conveniently, the three set down and shared the load. At about that point they some-how lost the trail to Panther Scald, and, while staving around looking for it, they began to hear strange and far-off music. Naturally they figured the music was from the dancing caper. So the three uplifters started bulging up a scrub-oak hillside that they reckoned would for sure lead to the meeting house.

But they were still blobbing along through the dense woods when they saw a shape standing clear in the early moonlight. It was a smallish little man with a big, hair-bushy head and a real whopper of a broadax draped over his left shoulder.

Deacon Cato sloshed up, spoke howdy, and asked was the little squirt chopping firewood, maybe boiler wood, for Erp's Canning Factory, and, if so, wasn't he working a bit late.

"Yes and no," the shape answered.

" 'Yes and no,' my tailbone," Cato snapped back, "Either you is or you ain't, so make up your mousy li'l' mind."

"I did that many years ago," the little feller said.

"Did what?'

"Made up my mind—to tend the trees."

"Who you chop for?" Kink inquired a bit sharply.

"Pan."

Tola yelled, "Pan? . . . What kind of a fool name is that? Pan of what? Fried mush? Catfish? Beefsteak? Scrambled eggs?"

"Just Pan."

"Never heard of nobody by that name, at least not nowhere hereabouts in these cultured, well-educated Arkansas Ozarks."

"First I ever heard of any peckerwood with a silly name like 'Pan,' " Tola chimed in. "How long you been workin' for him?"

"About twenty-one hundred years, I'd say."

Cato allowed the little squirt darn sure didn't care much what he was saying. Tola allowed that was for sure plenty long to woodpecker around on the same lousy choppin' job, and Kink takes on the questioning with, "What's your name?"

"Satyr."

"Satyr what?"

"Just Satyr."

About then the shape put in that he only chops into trees to free the spirits that gets left inside them. That there was carrying the silly talk too far. Up to then, Marcus and Tola and Cato all was figuring the little whoever was just too stuck-up to come right out and say he's only a plain ordinary peckerwood of a scrub wood chopper. But after that crack about freeing the spirits that got left inside trees, they figured for sure it was loose gravel between the ears.

When they commenced saying so, the Satyr just faded off into thick bushes, and when they set out to try learning the little whatever some manners, they didn't get anywhere except to a creekside mossbank that looks like a good place maybe to sit and take a breather, all recognizing there was still plenty of time to break up the dancing caper, and by now they were all of a mind to do a real good job of that.

But when the uplifters woke up again there was bright moonlight all around them. But even so, the place had a funny kind of first-timey look, and right off the uplifters begin hearing music again, except it don't sound like what goes with square dances. Like when a person gets that close to any back-hill dance on a Saturday night in Arkansas, he generally always hears feet stomping on floorboards long before he can make out any fiddle or git-tar or banjo or even plunket drums.

So anyhow, the three clodhoppers followed with their ears,

so to speak, until they come to a grove of tall sycamores where the music appeared by then to be coming from, only it turns out to be nothing like a square dance but something a lot more like on the order of a man singing an oddish song or two, then spelling out with maybe a flute solo.

Anyhow, the sound was real lively, and when it come to singing, the whoever-it-was could most outsing a martengale. The uplifters kept edging up closer, figuring by now maybe the young folks are rounding out their dancing antics with some tasty music. So they stood and listened for quite some spell before pushing on to bust up the party. They'd hardly moved a rod of space when they practically run into something that turns out to be the same little Satyr character. Only this time he'd left off his work jeans and hadn't put on nothing in their place except what looked like a four-bits strip of deerhide, but anyway, he was stepping around as spry and pert as a banty rooster headed for the henhouse. So Deacon Cato caught up and whammed him on the backside, remarking, "Cholly, for a feller twenty-one hundert years old, you look purty dang chipper."

Satyr thanked him kindly, and Cato went on to add he hoped he could count on being as full of spunk and vinegar when he passed twenty-one hundred, or, hell, just call it twenty hundred, even. But Kink cut in to comment that for any little quarter-pint squirt, even of a youngest twenty-one hundred years, to be prowling the night air without no breeches on was practically indecent besides asking for pneumony.

Then Deacon Cato asked sarcastic would it be all right for the three friends of virtue to step up closer to the orchestry on account they all relished good music. Satyr said he guessed that would be all right if they'd set still and behave theirselves, but he put it that what they had been hearing was no orchestry; it was the songs and pipings of the great Pan.

Tola caught on enough to belch out, "Oh, yeah. That there's the peckerwood you said you'd been workin' for. Fryin' Pan . . ."

He and Kink and Cato kept pushing up closer till they could see Satyr's boss face to face. Seems he was a youngish-looking character with long brown curly hair and didn't wear so much as a stitch of clothes except a mid-strip of maybe white buckskin that didn't look too indecent on account of only the upper half of the crittur was human, the rest being considerable like one of them newfangled mohair goats.

Anyway, there he or it sat, on a kind of brush pile, blowing into a flute that looked like maybe it was whittled out of a bamboo fishing pole, but anyhow, that *twee-twee* blowing was out of this world, and the more he blowed the closer the three uplifters got. Well, so finally, Cato couldn't hold hisself in no longer; he just rose up on his hind legs, capered a jig step, then switched into a old-time hoe-down stomp dance like he used to do when he was young and not yet uplifted to the Abiding Grace.

But just in that split second there came a great rush of breeze and noises like maybe a hundred pairs of bare feet scampering down the ravine, and the flute toots only once again. And next time the uplifters look around, they don't see anything or nobody till finally they see Satyr again. Only this time he don't seem nowhere near so friendly like, and he snaps out, "Why did you interrupt?"

The uplifters didn't like his tone of voice, the more so because that Satyr stood only hip tall to the shortest of 'em, same being Deacon Fietz, who sharped back, "We only come to hunt bullfrogs."

"A dry hillside's a sort of unlikely place to be frog hunting. I take it you like bullfrogs," Satyr mused out loud.

Cato flipped back, "Un-tall Shorty, next to the rightful and uplifted life, there practically ain't nothing we feel about so deep and tender as the hind legs of a big healthy papa bullfrog slow fried in sassafras-cured bacon grease——"

Satyr waited for a spell like he was maybe trying to figure out which was the calf's liver and which was the pig's, then he said, "I rather guessed maybe you came here with something else in mind, such as, for instance, like keeping the young people from having a happy frolic. . . . Or could I, maybe, be wrong?"

By then Tola was really waspy. "Could be you is wronger'n a Arkansas man wearin' socks. But come to think of it, a body couldn't hardly expect no loose-lugged, skin-headed peckerwood of an axman to be eggsactly right."

When Satyr didn't appear to pay special notice, the uplifters commenced to show quite a spiff of dander. Kink cuts in with, "Look, Cholly Boy, what if we be lookin' for bullfrogs, and what if we *ain't* lookin' for bullfrogs? How come it gets to be any of yore pukey business?"

About then, Deacon Cato commenced to warm up with the righteous fire and sets his left hand atop Satyr's head, saying, to wit, "Likewise, Buster, me and a-sociates ain't in the habit of bein' called liars by the likes of you——" His big right hand starts to hard into a fist. "Speakin' personal, I never yet before smacked nobody as old as you claim to be, but this here commences to feel like a first time. . . . That's for shore unless'n maybe you'd like to squat down and say, 'Purty please, I know for true you-all come here to ketch bullfrogs, and I hopes you ketch a barrulful.'"

So Satyr spoke back, "I hope you catch a barrelful." Except he didn't squat down. In place of that, he rose up straight and all at once his voice sharpened up like a town barber's best razor. "I more than hope you catch a barrelful," he went on, "I'm willing to let each one of you *be* a barrelful of bullfrog."

Just as Cato was letting go with a low-level haymaker, this Satyr wide-opened his funny eyes and snapped his fingers, like so. And you know what? Deacon Cato Fietz never finished his swing. Because Cato, same as Kink and Tola, was all at once hunkered down on the ground, and their eyes got bulgy and their goozles—that being the Arkansas word for what some would call their Adam's apples—started to puff in and out like with three big fat papa bullfrogs getting a close-up look at three big juicy waterbugs.

Then, all at the same time, all three of the uplifters tried to stand up and take out after Satyr. But straight off they all found out that they couldn't do nothing with their arms except flap them to and fro like in swimming, and all they could do with their silly legs was to squat down and hop.

When Cato Fietz tried to ask Satyr how come and what had happened, he couldn't for all goodness gracious get out so much as one word. All he could say was, "UMMMMMPH BAH!" When Kink and Tola started to get in their two-cents' worth, it commenced to sound like a frog-pond chorus comes Decoration Day.

When Satyr turned about and started strolling down a dogwood gulch, the three uplifters went bulging and plopping to follow him, but before they could frog-hop a dozen jumps, that Satyr was long gone out of sight.

Well, so the moonlight commenced to dim and fog started pushing up the deep hollers, and, after a lot of threshing and scratching through the thick bushes, the uplifters finally came to the footpath that truly did lead to the Panther Scald Meeting House. Only by then it had got mighty late, and anybody with eyes could see the dance frolic was closed out. But the ceiling lanterns still had warm chimneys, and there were fresh tracks on the trail that muddies along down to Catfish Creek.

So the three uplifters took out leapfrogging along through what was left of the moonlight, maybe reckoning that getting down to the big creek would be the rightest place left for them to go, all the more so because any three damn fools, even them, could see that there was where the young people had already went.

When the uplifters got to the swimmin' hole, they seen nine young females, leastwise they were acting like young, and seven young menfolks and the fiddle player, old crazy Wes Gordon from over around Nastyville.

So after the customary amount of silly shillies, the menfolks taken the deep pool past the tall grove of wild huckleberry bushes, and the womenfolks taken the sandy-bottomed pool directly near the pawpaw bushes. So you can just take and guess whichever swimming pool these three purifying uplifters went frogging into, but let me say here they wasn't seeking for no huckleberries.

All I need to say for sure is that those Tannehill twins, female, that is, was the first to shuck off and lay their underpretties on a drift log and go whapping stitchless into the water. Just as they began to just about wet their bellybuttons, Dellie said to Nellie, "Keep your silly hands to yourself!" And Nellie said back to Dellie, "Go stick your silly head into a pencil sharpener!"

By about then that tub-bottomed "Piggy" Suzie Lotten gal got to wading in her birthday suit, and all at once she turned around and squalled, "Somethin's pinchin' my——"

Little Truetta Heffelfinger come wading up to see what went on, only all at once she squealed and slapped, and the funny thing is she got slapped back, only nowhere near her face. By about the same time the Tannehill twins commenced to squeal again, and Dellie yelled to Nellie, "Stop pinching me, silly!" and Nellie yelled back, "Stop pinching *me*, silly!"

and Dellie yelled back, "I'm not pinching you, silly!" and Nellie yelled back, "I'm not pinching you, silly!" Both them girls was real quick and smart with their comebacks.

Just then, little Herbina Henson, who was floating on her backside, squealed out, "I see a great big whopper of a bull-frog. It's as big as Deacon Cato Fietz and most as ugly!"

So with that, little Herbina turned over and come splashing out, and the Tannehill twins come splashing out, and the fat Piggy gal comes splashing out. About that time, and one directly after the next, there sounded three big fat *kerplunks* in the deep, black-shaded water, and the rest of the females commenced to splash for the sandy bank, and by then the menfolks, in case you don't mind what you're saying, come over to see what was going on, and some of the gals squealed some more and went splashing back into the water again. Only there was some that didn't.

Around daybreak of Sunday, and all looking like they'd lately been rolled through a quicksand bog, Cato and Kink and Tola came bulging for the horse-watering trough right yonder in front of this here store, and, lo and behold, all three went frog-hopping into that slimy trough like they was born and raised there.

Next thing I see, when the church bell commenced to clang for meeting time, those three uplifters went frog-hopping right along to the services. For the opening hymn, Cato and Kink and Tola managed to keep squatted and fair quiet alongside the front bench. But when Pastor Pennington un-limbered his long, hairy, baboon arms and bore down about "brethren now is the hour for every true and transformed and purified spirit amongst us to jine hands in squenching the carnal flames that is seering the underpinnings of our younger generation," you couldn't help but see those three uplifters was all set to whoop out, "Amen!" But all any one or all three together could get out was, "UMMMMMPH BAH!"

The young people started to titter some, but Pastor Pennington went right on and nothing much elsewise happened till a big blue bottlefly commenced to buzz around the clear glass side window like as if it sure would enjoy to come in if'n it wasn't for that tarnal pane of winder glass in the way.

But what I really got to tell you is that when that big, silly bottlefly showed up, Cato, Kink, and Tola just set there looking frog-eyed, with goozles puffing in and out and tongues sliding to and fro. That there went on till sunshine hit that big fly just right for showing it up to be the fattest, juiciest, tastiest-looking bottlefly that ever bopped its fool head against any winder glass anywhere.

Then, all in the same swivet, preachin' or no, Cato and Kink and Tola rose up like one and the same bullfrog, and all three went plumping out the open door, all going hell-for-election after the same bottlefly, which took out for the tall timber and the far places.

Then somewhere out past Hawg-Eye Holler it come to pass that the three hunched-down uplifters met up with Satyr, who was back in blue jeans again and carrying his ax.

"How be the frogs?" he inquired.

Seeing they couldn't do nothing but puff and croak, Satyr stepped up closer, and finally he said, "I'm no teacher, but I even yet hope this here has taught you a lesson."

The little squirt wagged his head, then stepped back into the bushes, and, in maybe half the time it takes to pucker to whistle, he was gone again, and Cato and Tola and Kink was just standing there about as upright as ever and looking silly as normal.

I believed every word Cousin Leander had spoken; also that

the lock on the cookie bin would eventually yield. It did, and so, with six fig bars in my overalls pocket and two Queenie vanilla wafers in my mouth, I began probing for more of the higher truth.

"Has anybody seen Satyr since then?"

Lyin' Johnny's cousin-in-law lurched toward the front door and pointed an overlength forefinger toward a first fringe of sapling timber on the next to highest rim of Stick-up Mountain.

"See yonder blue speck about half the size of a monkey's tit the far side from where the persimmon grove points up like the topknot of a mad wet jaybird? Well, that there is Satyr. . . ."

"What's with Cato and Kink and Tola?" I inquired.

"Ever since that Sunday morn they've been their customary onery selfs."

"You mean they haven't changed at all?"

"Only their line of bizness, in case you choose to call anything those punks do a bizness."

"So what's their line of bizness now?" My accent was of pure synthetic vanilla.

Resignedly, Lyin' Johnny's cousin-in-law scooped up what was left of the fig bars. "All three is partnered together with a live bait farm for fishermen. . . . They've put their wives and young'uns to diggin' for red worms and ketchin' night crawlers, likewise fuzzy caterpillars and catalpa worms. . . ."

"Nothing uncommon about that, is there?'

"You might say there ain't." Lyin' Johnny's cousin-in-law pocketed the final remnant of the vanilla wafers. " 'Cept for just one thing. Those three uplifters gets brought in thousands and thousands of bugs and worms . . . but, anyhow, up till now they never had so much as one worm or one bug to sell nobody."

"How come?"

"I ask 'em all three that in those same words. . . . And all three speaking together give me the same answer."

"What did they say?"

Cousin Leander's cheeks were bulging with fig bars and truthful recollection.

"They said, 'UMMMMMMMMPH BAH!' "

HONEY HUNTER

During the 1870's, the decade of this story, the Ozarks abounded in agrarian trades and skills. One of the more engaging was "taking" wild honey. The pursuit fitted the subsistence economy of the earlier frontiers. For natural causes it endured well into the present century.

In my own youth, as recently as 1912–14, I had the pleasure of knowing several Ozarks honey hunters, including one who was most gratifyingly generous with his sweet caches. This young man was one of my Morrow-Ellis cousins. He took to honey hunting in the then flowery countrysides about Fayetteville, Arkansas. Ulley (I still cherish that name) Ellis earned enough from his honey hunting to pay for two years at the University of Arkansas. At the end of this period my cousin once removed was seized by the realization that bees, even wild bees, can be more interesting than tame professors.

Ulley's next adventure took him into a siege of collecting queen bees which he purchased from what he explained were respected apiaries. He assured his less literate kin that apiaries have no connection with apes, which, in turn, are not apiarists. With a velvet-lined bagful of superior queen bees, Cousin Ulley set out to the Pacific Northwest, then the most flowery region of the nation. When the professedly superior queen bee offspring encountered a dwindling of honey sources, Ulley replenished his collection of queens and set forth for ever flowering Central America, where in time he prospered from honey collecting until his affluence resulted in his being robbed and murdered by a pack of Panamanian thugs.

That, obviously, is another story, but it shares common roots with the Ozarks story here recounted. There was, in fact, a wild-honey hunter, his actual name was Michael Tileson, and he "honeyed" in the back hills of Taney County, Missouri. Though commonly described as a dwarf, he was about five feet tall. Even so, he was by no means the shortest man in his countryside; he had a kinsman at least a foot shorter.

The honey hunter was still in the "honey game" when, in 1911, he died of pneumonia, reportedly at the age of seventy-seven. He built up his own colony of beehives in the late 1890's. Michael was probably in his forties at the time of this story. I did not know Michael Tileson in person. However, while struggling along as an Ozarks correspondent for the *St. Louis Post-Dispatch*, I met many people who had been well acquainted with him; that year was 1924. Michael's cabin was still standing; he had lived alone in it until a few days before his death.

Unlike my cousin once removed, Michael lived in a country-side where the wildflower populations rarely failed the bees or the perceptive honey hunter. He was not afflicted with murderous banditti; he lived and died a "loner" with many friends. Even so, and in common with his far-back neighbors, Michael was harried by the Bald Knobbers, post–Civil War Ozarks kin of the original Ku Klux Klan, whose name was derived from their practice of building "mustering" fires on bare mountaintops or hilltops. Like the Ku Kluxers and similar conclaves of violent bullies, the Knobbers were nothing to be proud of.

It seems to me that Michael Tileson was. Certainly several of the countryside yarn spinners remembered him as a noble and worthwhile person, as well as the somewhat fabulous principal of a rather lengthy progeny of tellin' stories. What follows is of my own putting together as a popular magazine story. Even so— and there may be some who would be surprised to know this— it is partly true.

MICHAEL was a bee man, the best in all of Little Stony Valley. But Michael himself went no further than to admit that he was a "tol'able" bee man—his own word for "moderately good." None who knew him felt disposed to contradict or deny. But there were some who listed him not as a man, but as a dwarf. Others described him as just a forest-roaming boy who never grew up. Michael denied that estimate, pointing out that he was, in fact, past forty and tol'able tall; with his walkin' boots on, he stood five feet.

As for his age, Michael held that he was tol'able old—his hair was almost white—and tol'able young—still strong-gaited, sharp of eye, and quite effective with his razor-sharp hand ax, or, as need required, tol'able competent at climbing any honey tree, anywhere. Not many denied that Michael was somewhat better than tol'able at getting along with both people and bees, as needs required, simultaneously. He looked up to both.

In the case of wild bees, he began by locating their flight trails. Following these with tol'able skill led him to hidden stores of honey, usually in trees with hollow trunks. Once he located a honey tree, the honey hunter proved again that he was the tol'able or moderate kind. He would first locate the hive or "honey stand" and estimate its size by deftly tapping on the tree trunk and other reasonable ways.

When the honey stores were plentiful, Michael would use his hand ax to cut a vent and take out the wild honey. However big or small the find, the tol'able little man left at least half of the honey to feed the bee colony until it could recoup its stores. When summer droughts withered the fennel blooms and checked the blossoming of honeysuckles and myrtles and the valley flowers, Michael set out pans of sugar or cone honey near to the bee trees. When spring came late and summer droughts proved severe, Michael shared his very special and secret supply of queen bees so that the wild bees, as needs required, could divide their colonies and begin new ones where honey sources were more plentiful. It followed that the bees thrived and honey stores increased throughout the War Eagle country, in great part because Michael Sheehan was a tol'able honey hunter.

On a wooded hillside near War Eagle Village the honey hunter had chopped and hewn logs and built a cabin and chinked the logs with blue clay that he mined from a nearby creek bank. It was a one-room cabin, and the ceiling was tol'able low, so that a full-size man could not enter without stooping. But the interior was welcoming and clean, with pans and crocks and sparkling pewterware. The fireplace was small, but the hearth was well kept. Most of the time the mantelboard held bouquets of wildflowers or, in wintertime, sprays of mountain holly and buckthorn and cedar. But always the mantelboard held an immense yellow candle that was Michael's very special delight. For many years the big candle had kept its place of honor in the little room.

Life was generally kind in the Little Stony country, at least until the Bald Knobbers appeared. Then there came an evening when on his way home Michael saw a spiral of smoke rising from the village, and even from his doorway he heard a great shouting and presently a scurrying of hoofs.

While the uproar was fading into the greenish dusk, the honey hunter hurried to the village. He was in time to see Gladden's store in the course of being burned to the ground. The black earth about it was torn and scarred with hoofprints. And along the roadside he noted that tufts of wool hung from the roadside briars and thorn bushes; also that deep hoofprints led in the direction of the Red Star prairie. Anybody could see that the Bald Knobbers had raided, sacked the store, burned it, stolen the storekeeper's sheep and cattle, and driven them away. It was no tol'able act; Michael was deeply concerned.

Bald Knobbers?

They were the masked men, the night riders of older Ozarks times. The pillagers and dealers of unhappy surprises called together their scattered membership by building signal fires on bare hilltops. That accounted for the name "Bald Knobbers," but not for the evil deeds that the name had come to embody.

As he turned homeward, Michael stopped quickly, hearing a succession of light footsteps. They were Snowbelle's, the daughter of Matt Morrow, who kept the grain mill. She was young and pretty, and her eyes were bright, and first moonlight played over her wind blown hair. But her easy smile was gone, and her expression was one of distress and dread.

"Michael! The Bald Knobbers did dreadful things!"

"Wasn't even close to tol'able," the honey hunter agreed.

Snowbelle continued, "They took the storekeeper and all the village by surprise."

The honey hunter nodded. "For tol'able good folks, truly evil deeds always come surprisin'."

"And Eric has gone—down by the valley trail," the girl continued. "He figures the Bald Knobbers will be pasturing stolen sheep and cattle down in Red Star prairie. He says he will drive his father's livestock through the nearer ravine and turn them home again."

"A tol'able lad, that Eric Gladden. Maybe too much so for his own good." Michael paused thoughtfully. "He reckons all right. But I don't be sure he moves rightly."

"But the Bald Knobbers will take him over!" the girl exclaimed. "Unless you help him, he will never, never come back."

Michael felt Snowbelle's hand slip into his own.

"You will help him?" she asked.

"I'll try." He added slowly, "I'm an old man. They call me a dwarf and moon-struck. But I will try, young lady. For real and in my own little way, I'll try."

They walked together to the head of the lane that led to Morrow's mill. Rosebushes fringed the barricade of cedars; old tearoses and ramblers, some still crowded with late buds. Michael whispered. Snowbelle stooped quickly. She picked a rose, blood red and waxen, and pressed it into the honey hunter's hand. Then she left him.

Michael walked alone to his cabin. He laid the rose at the base of the great candle. Then he built a fire in the rock fireplace and made a supper of mealpone and mutton shoulder; then cleared away the pewterware. For a time he sat pondering.

Suddenly he started, fully awake. An uncertain square of light played upon the wall beyond his bed, shifted careeningly, came again. Michael stepped to the solitary window. Open fires burned on a bare hilltop to the west. Michael studied the fires; two high-flaming brush fires and between them a smaller one. The center fire vanished, then rose again. Presently all three sank to mounds of embers that shone in the darkness like magic buttons.

They were signal fires. From the looks of it, the Bald Knobbers were warning their members of invaders. New pillars of flame began rising and adding to the story. Michael watched until all the fires were dead. Then he dressed and made ready for the trail. First he slipped two pine faggots and a handful of matches into the side pockets of his jacket. Then he went out into the early moonlight. When he had come to the banked darkness of the millhouse, he whistled once. Snowbelle hurried to his side. They talked for a moment, then

Michael concluded: "If between now and morning the men-folks of the village decide to go after the Bald Knobbers, you go to my cabin and light the big candle and put it on the windowsill."

"I will."

Their hands touched, and the honey hunter went his way. He hurried across the narrowest tongue of War Eagle Valley and made for the far green slopes of West Mountain. When he came on the cattle path, he found it newly marked with hoofprints.

That was as he had guessed. The Bald Knobbers had driven the stolen cattle hard and downhill, following a course that even a hasty pursuer could see would lead to the great green prairie of Red Star. But Michael was no hasty pursuer. He knew that barely five miles from where he stood the trail divided. One fork meandered west into a succession of deep mountain ravines that led into the hill-cupped stronghold of the Bald Knobbers.

For a time the dwarf pondered the recent splatterings of hoofprints. And when he came to the fork of the trail, he turned abruptly and made for a labyrinth of limestone bluffs. He skirted the crests and headed toward a tree-plumed mountaintop. Painstakingly he climbed the great forehead of the mountain, and there listened until presently he heard the sound of trickling water. He followed the sound to a deep spring at the trail side. Around the spring were tumblings of limestone boulders. One after another the honey hunter began to view the rocks. Presently he stopped beside one of the smaller ones that was no more than a yard square. He broke a twig from a young oak tree and began scratching in the black earth beside the rock. Then he stooped low, and, slipping his hands beneath a corner edge of the stone, he raised it several inches.

At that moment, his straining hands felt the damp chilliness of enclosed air. He had located a cave entrance. The honey hunter was not surprised. He had learned long before that caves almost always had more than one entrance; as a rule, in limestone country every cave has several. The fine feat is in finding them.

Michael climbed down and then walked west again through dense fringes of underbrush and so crossed over the mountain and skirted down into the great grassland called Red Star prairie.

But within an hour's time he returned to the newly discovered back door of the cave. Again he lifted the heavy shatter of limestone, this time rolling it over. Certain that he had found a sure entry to a great cave, Michael struck a match to a pine stub that he carried in his jacket pocket. Then he crawled laboriously into a damp and narrow tunnelway that led into a great cave room.

As Snowbelle had predicted and Michael had foreseen, young Eric Gladden, the storekeeper's son, had walked squarely into a trap. As Michael had first guessed and later confirmed, the youth had trailed the stolen cattle to the forking of the trail. There he had followed the hoofprints into the grassy valley. But on the way, Eric had all but fallen over a Bald Knobbers' picket. Before the youth could turn around, the invaders were upon him.

One of the members laid hands on Eric's throat and, crushing him to the ground, bound his wrists with a hitching rope. Then, raising the youth, the Bald Knobber slapped his cheek. "So it was you they sent to find us out! How many more of your village punkies be follerin' you?"

Eric had answered quite truthfully, "I come alone by my own free will."

Thereupon, the tallest of the Bald Knobbers had pulled the youth before him and, with the help of the three other pickets, marched him to a mountaintop and down again to the outer rim of a high limestone bluff and stopped before a great door built of hand-hewn and weather-aged oak.

It was a door that opened into the very mountainside, more accurately, into a cave. The leader slipped a big bronze key into a round iron lock and laboriously turned the key. He strained hard, and presently the lock snapped, and the four Bald Knobbers joined in pushing open the big, heavy door.

"There's the place—Smarty Pip! So think back to your War Eagle town. You won't never see it no more!"

They pushed him through the doorway. There was a popping of sagging timbers as the great door was pushed shut. Then the renewed click of the lock. Eric, his hands still bound, found himself alone in pitiless darkness. He stumbled across a wet and rough floor of quartz. For hourlike minutes he endured the agonies of the cold darkness. But what could he do? Wander blinded into the chilling darkness? Farther back there would likely be chasms and fissures and maybe even quicksand. Vainly Eric tried to free his wrists. Then resignedly he began to wait through a cold and dark nightmare of silence.

After a time the youth started, struggled to rouse his benumbed senses. A glint of yellowish light played on high and jagged arches of cave ceiling. Presently Eric heard the faint, flattened vibrations of a footstep. Then, as if by magic, a balconylike projection of limestone hardly an arm's length above his head lifted into a dazzling light. And leaning over a balustrade of prisms, Eric saw a dwarfish figure who held in one hand the hard-used stub of a pinewood torch.

It was Michael. The honey hunter made his way down an embankment of dripping rock. Still holding the burning stub of pine, he took a jackknife from his pocket, opened the blade, and with one deft slash freed Eric of his bonds. Then he drew another pine stub from inside his jacket and painstakingly lighted it from the first.

Wonderingly, Eric fondled his free hands. "Thanks ever and ever so much, Michael. But I don't understand."

"Neither do the Knobbers," Michael answered easily. "Some say a cave is like a woman's heart. I wouldn't truly know about that, but I would know there's generally more than one way of getting into a cave. In limestone country caves have back doors and side doors the same as front ones. So I came in the back door—from the far side of the mountain. It's been all of forty years since last I was through this cave." Michael winced and raised his free hand to Eric's shoulder. "And now we must get out by the back door. So keep close to me, lad. And watch out for the quicksand."

Michael led the way down tortuous lanes of sleek quartz to steep paths of schists and alabaster. Presently they came to a still stream and waded its icy water. Michael laboriously skirted gray-black pits of quicksand, then led the way into the narrow blackness of the vent tunnel. Eric stumbled outside into a near jungle of tall sedge grass.

"Rest a spell, lad! It's still before midnight."

"Night?" Eric asked in amazement.

"Aye, time passes underground the same as above it."

Eric rubbed his eyes, then looked up at the stars and the waning moon. "You saved my life. What might I do to pay back?"

"The debt is not to me." The honey hunter smudged out the remnant of his pine torch, then led the way, walking rapidly down the mountainside. After they were back to the river valley, the older man stopped again and pointed. After long gazing, Eric, too, made out a dim, flickering light.

"The light flickers, lad. It's the big candle in my cabin. The young lady was to light it and set it before the window in case the War Eagle men went after the Bald Knobbers. Candle says they're gone already. Likely they went out to find you and take back the stolen livestock. But they'll do neither."

Eric's voice had the ring of derring-do. "We could join with the War Eagle men, go with them into the Red Star valley, and help take back the sheep and cattle."

Michael shook his head. "Better to spend the time at other work. I take it our people went by way of Weddington Gap. That, of course, is the long way and the wrong way. Fact is, that's likely just what the Knobbers expected and wanted them to do. The trip by Weddington Gap way will take them all the night; and most of tomorrow—likely *all* of tomorrow." Michael nodded thoughtfully. "Now, there's no menfolks left at War Eagle Village to keep watch on homes and livestock, what's left of the sheep and cattle, that is——"

Eric's concern was evident. "Expect they'll raid in full daylight tomorrow. Like you know, sheep and cattle drive easier in daylight. And the Knobbers will likely drive farther next time. And now that all the menfolks are gone from the village and around it, home doors and pasture gates will open easier. Untol'able is untol'able," he concluded.

"But what about the sheep and cattle they already stole? Who will be guarding them?"

Michael smiled. "There's none left to guard." He nibbled a twig of sassafras. "You see, lad, before I came after you, I see the Knobbers had built a stockade of split rails likely stolen off somebody else's fences down in Red Star prairie." He paused solemnly. "So before I came for you in the cave, I strolled over to that stockade and pulled down a span of the fencin' so as to let the sheep and cattle get free." Like you know, livestock finds ways to get home same as people. Comes noontime tomorrow, your pa's sheep and cattle will be straggling back to home pastures——"

"But what about the Knobber pickets?"

"They had set their pickets, all right . . . the same ones you stumbled into. But I skirted around 'em. And I foretell that, comes the daylight, those mighty heroes will have a real surprise waitin' for 'em."

"How you know the stolen sheep and cattle are outside the stockade?"

"On account I drove 'em out. . . . The stockade's smallish and the herds wasn't exactly big . . . eighteen cattle as I recollect it, and close to thirty sheep."

"That was all we had," Eric said.

"All carried your brand," Michael answered. "And before tomorrow's over, they'll come straggling home. . . ." The old man glanced to the east. "But sooner than that, unless I miss my guess something mighty—the Knobbers will be back to War Eagle Village, raiding again. The trick's as old as sin itself. Pillage, lure off the defenders, then come back, and pillage more and worse."

Eric spoke quickly "Then, it's your notion for you and me to go back to the village?"

The honey hunter nodded, this time with great emphasis.

The east was brightening when Michael and Eric turned up the road to War Eagle Village. A first salute of smoke was rising from the millhouse chimney. As the two early travelers neared the miller's cottage, a light figure in blue gingham ran toward them. It was Snowbelle. She smiled at the honey hunter, and the smile told of great thankfulness. The girl turned quickly and leaped into Eric's outstretched arms.

Michael looked on thoughtfully; then he strolled across the roadway to a nearby slope of hillside where he peered intently at a large oak tree that grew alone. Then he turned back, again glanced quickly at the boy and girl, and hurried into the shadow-crowded pathway that led to his cabin.

Inside, the flat rock hearth was long dead of fire. The big candle was burned to a whitish puddle of tallow that waited on the window sill. But the rose Snowbelle had given him was still bright red and gay.

Michael dabbed his hands and face with cold water from an earthen basin. Then, with deference, he approached a screen-covered case that held a place of honor in the chimney corner. With great care the honey hunter opened the top drawer and counted out twelve small cups, each made of flannel and covered with a screening of thin muslin. He handled them most carefully, for each cup held a queen bee, long and slender and shiny black.

Carefully he placed the twelve cups in a silken bag, which he hung on a lilac bush just outside the doorway. Then he looked up toward the line of treetops, and presently he heard a great whirring of bees. Within minutes the tall lilac bush was darkened with increasing throngs of bees. The honey hunter stepped cautiously beyond the swarming bush and noted that the cabin walls were also splotched with bees. Then he walked hurriedly to a thatch-roofed shed that sheltered neat tiers of home-built boxes, each one roofed and holed for use as a beehive.

He lifted down twelve of the hive boxes and raised the top boards of each. He buttoned his jacket tightly and pulled his cap low over his eyes. Cautiously Michael reapproached the ever increasing swarms of honey makers. Very slowly he lifted down the silken bag, and, one after another, he took out the velvet cups, and, moving very slowly, he placed one "throne" or queen bee in each of the hives.

Then, still moving very cautiously, he picked up two of the boxes, one under each arm, and carried them, with swarming bees following, and placed the boxes at the roadside, across from Morrow's mill. That done, he trotted back to his cabin and again carried two more boxes to the roadside before the mill. He made four more trips, each time returning in great haste but carrying the boxes slowly and with respectful caution.

The village wives and children were more than a little puzzled by the moves of old Michael Sheehan and his reasons for bringing on so great a swarm of bees at the roadside. They were even more puzzled when the honey hunter, with the help of young Eric, began to chop down the lone oak tree on the rise immediately above the roadway. For certainly it was not a honey tree. But the women and young ones had much else to wonder about, including the fortunes or misfortunes of their menfolk who had gone forth against the Bald Knobbers. The signs were not good. A whippoorwill kept calling from nearby, an omen of bad trouble. But none questioned the honey hunter and Eric Gladden as they continued their peculiar work.

Meanwhile, the honey hunter and his youthful helper felled the big tree on the slope paralleling the road. They cleared the great body log of its limbs and chopped off the treetop. They placed a smaller log beside the great trunk, apparently to serve as a fulcrum. Then they cleared a long and straight tree limb, making it into what appeared to be a pry-pole.

Having finished the work, the honey hunter viewed the increasing swarm of bees. Then he stood very still, listening intently. Presently the honey hunter heard a distant clattering of hoofs and the murmuring of men's voices, which became more guttural as they came nearer.

The Bald Knobbers were coming again. Within a very few minutes the raiders were in full view. There were sixteen in all, most of them big men, somber and menacing. Some carried muskets, others swung herding whips. When they came to the scant barricade of logs and bee boxes, the leaders hesitated.

Michael and Eric, standing manfully behind the oak log, commanded them to halt. For a moment the Bald Knobbers stopped, marveling at the audacity of the little old man and the teen-age boy. Then, with a flurry of oaths and jeers and derisive laughs, they came on.

As the invaders approached, Michael lifted the pry-pole in place and climbed upon it. Eric hurried to join him, leaped high, and so put the last ounce of his strength and weight on the high end of the pole. The fulcrum log sank. The pry-pole popped threateningly, then straightened and held. The great oak log moved perceptibly and made a part turn. The pry-pole sank lower, and all in an instant the great log rolled and bounded down the slope.

The invaders shouted and spurred and wheeled their horses in order to get out of the way of the log. There was a shot and a continued scrambling for safety as the big log sped down into the roadway. Then, with a smashing impact, it crashed into the barricade of bee boxes.

That brought forth a mighty roar of tens of thousands of wings as stinging torrents of outraged bees made upon the invaders. The Bald Knobbers beat a frenzied retreat, meanwhile striving to fight the bees from their faces.

Michael waited until the last of the Bald Knobbers, swollen-faced and half-blinded, was routed. The Bald Knobbers never came back to War Eagle. And so a dwarfish honey hunter and a teen-age youth saved a village.

It was after sunset when the menfolk of War Eagle returned, hard-worn and bedraggled. The sheep and cattle earlier stolen from the storekeeper had lagged and browsed their way home considerably earlier. Then the War Eagle people raised a purse to reward the honey hunter. But Michael gave the purse to the storekeeper whose establishment had been destroyed and asked that he use the money toward rebuilding the store. Then, when all the thanks were spoken, Michael walked with Eric and Snowbelle to the millhouse.

The girl spoke first: "But somehow we must pay you back."

Michael smiled, and his lips seemed very old. "But it is not me you owe. It is life. And all the happiness and all the wonders life keeps for the two of you that are young and in love. That's of the tol'able way."

When they had parted, Michael found his cabin waiting and welcoming. He piled dry wood in the fireplace and turned to the solitary window. It held only a withered red rose and the melted remnant of what had been the big candle.

RED RAMBLER

The time of this story is the latter 1860's, for much of the Ozarks the somewhat belated heyday of stagecoach travel. Most of the "taverns" along principal stage routes were farmhouse hostelries for accommodating the passengers as "mealers" or "overnighters." Few were taverns in the prevailing meaning of catering places serving liquor and its imbibers. In most instances the stagecoach hostelries were roadside residences in which home-set tables and fireplace-heated lobbies or "parlors" were provided, with complementary yardway facilities such as washing tubs, horse-watering troughs, privies, and stables. It followed that the "stop-over" taverns had much to do with making long-haul stage travel endurable and the facility at least occasionally solvent.

The most competent of the interstate stagecoach runs in the Ozarks was for almost a quarter of a century sustained by the Butterfield Stage Lines which "operated" all the way to San Francisco. Its Ozarks routes ran from St. Louis to Springfield and southwest to Fort Smith, Arkansas, a long-time outpost of the United States Army. Its throughway included the principal "wire roads," i.e., those with telegraph lines.

Butterfield drivers and section bosses alike were keenly appreciative of both the importance and the vagaries of the tavern keepers on whom they were so dependent. Understandably, one-time Confederate Colonel Cassius X. (for Xerxes) Hatfield used to tell me about stagecoach tavern keepers he knew. The Colonel knew most of the "stops" prevailing at the time of this story; he had been a Butterfield Stage driver for several years before the Civil War and a "boss driver" for nine years subsequently. The Colonel vowed that the most neighborly and most "peculiarest" people he had known were the roadside tavern folk. Partly in substantiation, he told me the gist of the ensuing story of the Matron Dodd, her wild son, her queer son, and the "bounden" girl.

SYLVIA lay on a straw pallet reveling in the morning sunlight that filtered through the long-unwashed attic window. She presently aroused sufficiently to finish eating an apple that she had cached in her blouse. That accomplished, she combed her long and silken black hair. Next she got to her feet and with deliberateness stepped to the narrow window and looked down on the great hedgerow of newly blooming locust trees that marked the upper maw of War Eagle Valley.

From the general direction of the driveway, which joined the stage road shortly beyond the sentinel locusts, she heard a snatch of song:

> Beefsteak when I'm hongry,
> Corn licker when I'm dry—
> Purty li'l gal when I'm lonesome,
> Sweet heaven when I die ....

The song continued. The voice was young and vibrantly masculine. As it came closer, Sylvia caught a glimpse of a bright green cap with a long white feather in its tip. From improved vantage she next saw a tall young man dressed in home-woven gray woollens and a buckskin jacket. Still singing rather loudly and walking with long-strided grace, the youth sprang over a holly hedge and vanished into the front entrance of the Steer Horn Tavern.

Smiling, Sylvia stepped back from the window and

stretched her arms, then rested her shoulders on a sector of gray-plastered wall that the early April sun had warmed. When a woman is nineteen and pretty and has a lover and it's springtime . . . .

Next, she heard steps on the stairway directly below, heavy steps, and with them an audible swishing of heavily starched skirts. Sylvia had expected the intrusion; she had also dreaded it. Funny thing about that old cow of a tavern mistress; she wore so many petticoats she always appeared to move as if mounted on casters. Except, of course, when she came to a flight of stairs. Like now . . . Madame Dodd was confronting her second flight of stairs and talking to herself quite audibly.

"Late mornin' a'ready. And not a dish washed. Not a kettle on the stove. House a ungodly mess! Damn me, just wait till I git my hands on that lazy hussy. I indentured her out of jail. Feed her like a fattenin' hawg. . . . Christ Jesus, it's most time fer the early noon stage. . . . God-be-mighty, I believe I hear it now. Dinner people, anyhow. And this here's a tavern without so much as a spot of warmed water. . . . That shiftless bitch . . . Done paid her bondin' money. Payin' her extry four bits a week fer workin' wages. . . . Sylvy, answer me! And don't dare to pull that caper of hidin' out because my eyesight is porely!" The strident voice reached a grating climax. "So there you be! Pretendin' ails again? Well, so now I be fetchin' you med'sin."

Madame Dodd moved forward menacingly, crowding the doorway with her massive body. "A purty sight you do make—comes the highness of noon." Sylvia was retreating toward a far corner.

"I ain't hearty today, Missus Dodd. That's how come I oversleeped. But I'll settle to work now. I'll ketch up."

The matron's low forehead was deeply puckered. Her neck veins, like her eyes, were bulging. She banged shut the door.

"You is already ketched up. First thing I'll have you to do is shuck off that there sleepin' gown and front yourse'f to that wall."

The girl's arms shaped a gesture that seemed to begin in defiance and ended in supplication. "I'm a growed-up woman, Missus Dodd, most twenty year old. And I won't be whupped no more. I—I jest won't stand fer it."

"You don't got to stand for it, only for long enough to git stripped off that nightie gown."

As Sylvia obliged, the tavern mistress moved across the attic. "I done hung a whup strap in yon closet. Better it be there. So it is. . . . Now, you git yourself down astraddle that there floor crack."

"Oh, Ma!" The voice that called from the stairs landing was almost like a child's, but its pitch was as unchanging as a mature man's. "Ma, the stage is here. People's gettin' off. Looks like lawyer mens from Fayetts-vul."

"For the dirty land's sake!" Matron Dodd completed a first fierce swing of the heavy strap. Sylvia cried out and scrambled forward.

The big woman paused very reluctantly. "You stay put and don't move a trifle and don't yell out no more. This time, young lady, you gits all you got comin' and more fer to recollect on."

Madame Dodd began picking her way down the heavily shaded stairs. In the big kitchen her eldest son had climbed back into his oversized highchair, where he was laboriously chewing a ginger cake.

"Are they here yit?"

The dwarf swallowed hard. "Jist now a-lighted."

Amos resumed his nibbling. No fit way for a man turned thirty to act? Maybe not, but Amos Dodd was not truly a man. He was still a shade short of being four feet tall. Only his head and chest were big. Otherwise, he was sized like a six-year-old, yet already stooped and graying like a man of fifty.

When his mother had moved out toward the entrance drive, Amos cautiously climbed down from his chair. Sylvia had come into the kitchen. She was beautiful, and for him she was the maker of new dawns.

"Amos, tell me, where is your brother Robin?"

The dwarf's head sank and his lips curved downward in evident disappointment. "Why should I know? He just now come in. Said he was going up to the sage pasture to look about the sheep. But how could *I* know where he truly went?"

Sylvia stood close, watching the dwarf intensely. "Do try to remember." Stooping quickly, she kissed him. Amos straightened as if in a rhapsody of delighted surprise. For the moment he held to her skirts.

"Amos, you have to save me!"

"I—*I* have to—"

"From your mother, Amos. If Robin were here, I know he could. Your mother is going to whip me again."

"You?"

"Yes, Amos. With that awful big harness strap. She hit me only once, but that one lick left a welt most as red as a strawberry. Should she go on, I'll get peeled down to bare bones."

"What you do bad?"

"Nothin'. True to God, nothin'. I was only there ladyin' in the attic an' she come all in a fury an' said I'd been shirkin' my work. But real an' true, I haven't been. Amos! Here she comes back. You mustn't let her——"

"For you I would——" An oversize shadow moved toward the outer doorway. The dwarf stumbled forward and, with his small, ill-shaped hands, grasped his mother's skirts.

"Ma! You are all wrathy mad——"

"The saints amongst us!" The keeper of the tavern waited toweringly, raising a hand as if to slap the dwarf's cheek. "Don't you stand there and tell me how to mind my business! *My* business . . . and me wearing my tired, old fingers to the bone to keep a roof above our heads and food in our bellies— your head, Amos Dodd, and likewise, your belly! I take on that good-for-nothing hussy there, pay her my good money, feed her my good victuals, have my house messed and be- fouled with her clutter and worthlessness. So now comes the stage. No horse water, so I got to fill up the trough. No washin' water, so I got to skim down to the big spring to fetch it—and it cold as old slop. No dinner yet set, nor even cooked. Customers waitin' in a still undusted parlor room. And you tell *me*——"

"But you agreed to look after Sylvy like as if she was one of your own."

"One of my own! Had I of handled her like my very own daughter girl and she carried on such a way like she has and does, I'd a seed to it long ago that she had no bottom end left for to set on!"

"Ma, it's tiredness and wrath that moves your tongue." With an oddly slow smile Amos bore the ensuing tirade. When it was ended, he spoke with rather astonishing firm- ness. "Sylvy is growed up now—to a fine, pretty woman."

With great effort the dwarf reached into his jacket pocket and brought out two half-dollars. He handed them to his mother. "That there is Sylvy's pay for two weeks—pervided you don't bedevil her no more."

In deep astonishment Matron Dodd fingered the coins. "So, ain't you the li'l ladies' man?" Then to Amos's evident surprise, his mother began to laugh. "I says again when money comes free—like the wild berries you pick, or the wild-bee honey you snitch, or the muskrat pelts you get trapped—I takes it. But I don't change my aims." She glanced meaningfully at Sylvia. "I'm tellin' you fair and square, the split second we finish up with dinner, and her helpin', that fond young lady of yourn gets the rest of what I only jist now started."

Almost playfully she lifted Amos back into his highchair. "Set yourself till dinner's cooked." She scowled at Sylvia. "And you get to hustlin'!"

Amos found himself without lust for the midday meal. Maybe the ginger cake had spoiled his appetite. Maybe the parting with his money had dulled his craving for food. But his greatest worry was for Sylvia. Try as he had to buy her out of it . . . .The diners were finishing their bout with plates and pewter. He saw Sylvia valiantly busy at the dish tub. But it wouldn't do her any good. As soon as the customers were out of hearing range his Ma would . . . Amos couldn't bear to think of it. And he wouldn't just sit and listen through.

Desolately the dwarf pushed aside his serving of beef hash and potatoes and with great caution climbed down from his highchair. He would try to disrecollect. He would walk himself away from the hateful, hurtful thing.

As the stagecoach moved out, the dwarf picked his way down the rock steps and went forth into the early afternoon. First he strolled to the nearer pasture where a dozen or so of his brother's sheep were grazing the newing grass. At least, Robin claimed they were his sheep. But were they? Amos looked more closely at a heavily fleeced black-faced ram. How could his brother have bought or swapped fair for this fancy crittur? The little man waddled on across the pasture, picked his way through an entangling grove of young persimmon trees, and pushed on to Carpenter's Creek. Quite deliberately he peered down at his reflection in the mirror-clear pool. And at least for a moment what he saw was not the image of a ludicrously little man with a grotesquely big head and chest, but that of a tall, sun-bronzed young man with a handsome face—surprisingly like his brother Robin's.

After a reflective pause the dwarf began to pick his way along the creek's course. He presently located his own very private trail that led around a great entanglement of sumacs and presently ended at a most engaging moss bank. Here, for sure, was a perfect spot for a man, even a stove-up runt of a man, to have himself a rest-nap. The green-golden afternoon was right for it, and whatever else was set to happen, well—it damn sure would happen.

Amos awakened quite abruptly, aware that he had napped considerably longer than he had intended, but, much more concernedly, he was aware of approaching footsteps. Hurriedly, but almost soundlessly, the dwarf retreated into a nearby fringing of wetland reeds that separated the moss bank from a knoll well screened by creekside willows. From that vantage, as the little man had learned long before, he could look down at the moss bank without being seen. He was confident, too, that the short, velvety moss would show neither his footprints nor the imprint of his body.

Even so, Amos rather resented the approach of the trespassers. The moss bank was of his most special little world; precious few others knew of it. He could recall with certainty only one other who knew his very own moss bank; that one was his brother. Many years before, when Robin was only a toddler and Amos was a stunted twelve-year-old—by then he was already at his tallest—he had taken Robin to the moss bank and, for no real reason, shared with him his very special shrine.

Of the two voices and the two sets of footsteps, Amos could identify almost certainly the one that belonged to his brother. Almost instantly, as he had also guessed, the dwarf saw that

Sylvia was with Robin. Arm in arm, the two were matter-of-factly invading the moss bank. What surprised the hiding watcher most was that Sylvia had survived her whipping remarkably well. She was, in fact, smiling, and her beautifully rounded face seemed more radiant than he had ever seen it before.

Both youngsters moved confidently, and their young voices seemed to dance out through the sleepy air. But when Robin motioned her to sit, Sylvia, for the first time, shook her head. "I can't, honey sweet. My setter is all gummy with blood. But if you will tell me to, I'll lay down on my side."

Quite purposefully, Robin was lifting her skirts. "Then, I'll tell you to. Fact is, I'll make you to."

With great caution the girl was sinking to the moss bed. "Please don't smack me no more, dear lovely. I'll be ever so good. But I'm so dreadful stiff and hurty. That was the most awfullest whuppin' I ever got. And I've sure took a-plenty of 'em."

The youth was beside her, caressing her breasts. "From me you might be gettin' plenty more."

"From you I wouldn't mind. I'd even might cherish gettin' whupped." She added in painful reminiscence, "But from your Ma . . . She shore to God did peel and blister my backside. And don't tear off my underpurties. They is all the ones I got left. . . . That pore li'l Amos," she mused, "he tried so hard and gave over his money, and . . . ."

"That pore li'l Amos is the tryin' sort. But it all goes for naught."

"He gave up most all the money he had for me."

Robin paused briefly. "Come to recollect, it was him that first showed me this here moss bank. Sorta too bad he won't never know what it's most usefulest for."

"Dearest heart, after you get through with showin' me what it's best usefulest for, then what will we do?"

"I'll tell you when I'm tired out on you. I got notions. . . . Only for now, I got still better ones."

For a time Amos gazed up into the willow tops. Then, still disdaining to look, he heard his younger brother's voice. "You'll wait here whilst I go fetch and hitch up my team wagon and stash hit afore them locust rises and tie down and load them fancy Cots'al rams and ewes I been borrowing the loan of from the Crumps and Adamses down past Ginger Blue. I'll leave the rest of my sheep agrassin'. When all's set, I'll come back and sashay you to where the wagon's at. With you up front and the sheep in back we'll take off for them far places past Greasy Creek."

"Do I got to walk far? I'm so hurtful sore——"

"You'll walk like where I tell you to. First off, we'll wade this creek times enough so as no dawg or no sheriff man will ever kitch our trails."

"But dear heart, I'm so terrible sore——"

"I ain't made done with you yet. And you'll always and forever be doin' what I tell you to."

"Yes, honey sweet, course I will. Only what about the law men?"

"What about the law men? Comes tomorry, we'll be far gone in new country, with plenty fine sheep for to sell and no clodhoppin' shirt badges a-taggin' us."

Amos waited in aching loneliness, his stubby hands rammed deep into his jacket pockets. Both pockets were almost empty now. In the right he could feel only a half-dime and four coppers; in the left only a mussel shell. If only he had back his big silvers. In retrospect they seemed as big and beautiful as a new moon. And not much easier to lay hands on.

"Chore time, you chigger!" Madame Dodd was forthright in her questioning. "Where you been hidin' out so long? 'Taint like you. And you ain't been lately asleep. Your eyes is wide like a hoot owl's. Now, tell your Ma, what pesters you?"

Two dwarfed legs dangled desolately from the bedside as the mother continued to interrogate. "You fearful you get cow-kicked should you try to milk? Well, I'll stand aside you and set a pole to shy off the cow kicks. 'Twon't take you long. ... 'Taint your rightful job, but that hussy Sylvy ain't showed. Soon as she does, I'll take on with that piece of harness leather where I left off. Milkin's her job. This time she sneaked off, but she'll be sneakin' back. When she does——"

"Sylvy ain't comin' back."

Madame Dodd patted the big, tousled head. "She'll come back. I know her kind. Bein' woman, I know what way to handle womankind. Don't fret your head about her no more."

"It's Robin I'm fretted about."

Madame Dodd patted the big, tousled head. "She'll come brother's growin' into natural manhood. It ain't natural that you should understand the likes of wenchin' and lickerin' and makin' jokes with constables and such like."

Amos was not placated. "You know what I mean as full well as I do. Robin steals sheep."

Madame Dodd frowned darkly. "Who says?"

The dwarf reached disconsolately for a heavy wooden milking bucket. "Who needs say? Only past this noontime I looked at the sheep in the near pasture. There alone stand more sheep than Robin ever owned. I see a fancy Cots'al blackface ram unlike anything that ever growed up around these parts before. And I see brand marks new changed—like two ear slits made into three with a side notch put on for to make 'em look like Robin's brand. And——"

Madame Dodd was raising a large hand in protest. "Don't set there and speak evil of your brother. How many times already have I told you, like the Holy Scriptures says, you be your brother's keeper?"

"I'm strivin' to be that."

"And should a lamb stray from the flock——"

"Ma, what I'm special talkin' about ain't no lamb. And it hasn't strayed from no flock. It's a full-growed ram, and it was stole. And it ain't the only such a one on this here place. And I'm expectin' the law is already found out."

Madame Dodd fidgeted uneasily. "But, Amos, honey, that there lazy-tailed sheriff man from Hunterville wouldn't never come out this far. Neither would that silly apple-headed constable man from Ginger Blue."

Amos was unconvinced. "Constable Erp was by here and pasture checking, most two weeks ago. I hear tell Sheriff Tatum's all hot and pestered."

"You truly think them law men might come *here*?"

"Nothin's shyin' 'em off. I get the feelin' they could be comin' this very night."

For the first time, Madame Dodd's uneasiness was apparent. "Amos, keep ever in mind . . . you be your brother's keeper."

The dwarf buttoned his frayed jacket and reached for the milk bucket. "Don't bother 'bout comin' along, Ma. I ain't fearful 'bout gettin' cow-kicked."

When he returned from milking, the dwarf went to the buttry shelf. When he was certain that he was not being watched, he picked his way silently from the big kitchen to the unlighted storage room beneath the front hallway stairs.

Amos waited until he was quite certain that he heard his mother flouncing in her bed directly overhead; then with great caution he took down the oil lamp from its table rack and placed it on the floor of the storage room. With the help of the less than generous light, the purposeful searcher located a hand ax, felt its cutting edge approvingly, and placed the tool next the doorway. Then with equal care he located and removed a ready-measured fifty-foot roll of shearing cord, actually a light rope about a quarter-inch in diameter and most frequently used for binding fleeces of newly shorn wool. In the nearest corner he edged toward an earthenware stand with a tightly placed lid. Directly over it hung a cluster of hollow cattle horns. Amos took down the largest of them and, straining manfully, removed the heavy lid to the earthenware stand.

Then he painstakingly filled the horn with the black, sulfur-odored gunpowder. With deft care he set the powderhorn, butt end up, next to the hand ax. Next he located a clay pot filled with already cut scraps of heavy cotton cloth. He removed a handful from the pot and rammed them into his jacket pocket. Then he filled his other pocket from a bowl of lead shot, some almost half the size of a sewing thimble. He picked his way through the clutter and heavier shadows until he stood beneath a long-barreled flintlock musket that hung on a rack made from two moldering sets of deer antlers. With deft stealth, the dwarf placed an empty tool chest below the antler rack and, straining hard, lowered the oversize musket.

By the feeble lamplight he looked carefully to the flints and the two slightly rusted hammers. Then he loaded the weapon. With the long ramrod that had been placed beside it, he thrust in a first wadding of cloth, then poured the hornful of gunpowder down the muzzle, tamped it in, and poured in the pocketful of shot, tamping it down. Moving as if each step were his last, the dwarf began carrying the well-chosen accouterments through the darkened hallway and placing them directly beside the front door. After he had replaced the smoky oil lamp in its rack and closed the storeroom door, he stepped outside into the settling night. At that moment he heard, from the front gable of the great roof, the night cry of a bird. Unhappily, Amos recognized the call of a whippoorwill, which, if made from the roof of a peopled house, surely foretells death. But the dwarf accepted the omen; what had to be would be; if death came, it would be a purposeful coming. For Amos Dodd was his brother's keeper. He was obliged to shelter his baby brother from an invasion by the lawmen. To accomplish that, he would set a protective trap. When quite certain that Robin and Sylvia were well on their way, he would take away the trap.

Heavily laden, the dwarf picked his way out into the gathered night. There was already moonlight on the hilltops, though the valleys remained dark with great silence.

Amos stealthily made his way to the dark curve where the tavern driveway joined the main road. There, as he clearly recalled, stood two sentinel trees, one an oak, the other a tall locust. Amos propped the musket against the nearer oak, and began placing the cording rope across the narrowing of the main road. Using his hand ax deftly, he felled a sapling and chopped its slender body length into four yard-long stakes. He sharpened them and drove the first two into the center of the roadway. Then at a height of about eighteen inches, he carefully circled the stobs with the thin rope. That done, he drove the two remaining stobs into the wet ground quite near the oak tree, shaping with them an $\times$ for supporting the musket barrel. Then having pressed aside an impeding stand of tall grass, he painstakingly placed the butt of the big musket against the base of the oak tree. That accomplished, he began to laboriously unravel the farther end of the small rope. In the freed strand he shaped a slip knot and strung it carefully about the trigger of the musket. Next, with exquisite care he pulled back the firing hammer in final readiness.

Then, he rechecked the tautness of the rope line and the tension of the slip knot. With almost breathless care he made certain that the musket was aimed directly across the roadway. That done, he once more checked over his handiwork and re-straightened the tall tufts of grass near the base of the oak tree. Alertly he looked down the road.

Whoever came, whether afoot, on horseback, or by carriage, would not come any great distance farther; at least not until Amos Dodd chose to so permit.

The regrettably little man recovered his hand ax and for a long minute stood peering into the night. He set to recalling the conversation of the love-makers on the moss bank. Surely by now the pair were wagoned and on their way. But Amos resolved to make sure. At least in a general way, he knew where Robin had hid the ready-hitched wagon and its cargo of stolen sheep. He would next find the place and make certain that Robin and his liftings had moved out. If the team and wagon were still there, he would return and watch the trap until he was quite certain that Robin and Sylvia had made their getaway.

Now that moonlight was taking over, the looking would be easy. Again the dwarf readied himself for walking. As he headed for the near pasture, he was annoyed to find that the moonlight was being dimmed by a rapidly invading river mist—so very dense that it slowed a man's progress and caused even the known countryside to seem strange and mixed-up like. Any ordinary man would almost certainly be getting himself lost. But Amos Dodd was no ordinary man. And what he did was no ordinary doing.

Determinedly he made his way to the dimming outline of the staggered rail fence. He would follow the fence line to the first foothill. There, beyond the line of locusts, he would find the markings of where Robin's wagon had been or, just possibly, still waited.

An owl hooted from the lower valley. From a nearby hedge came a strange intermixing of bird song. What kind of birds were these? Maybe there was due cause for listening. Somewhat dazedly the dwarf turned about. But the next sound he heard was from behind him. From the direction of the narrowing roadway he heard the great jolting roar of a musket shot.

It was—had to be—his man-trap.

Almost sobbing for breath, Amos turned about and retraced his course along the wavery fence line. He began trotting through the great crescent of the lower pasture; then, with heart pounding and chest aching, he managed to find his way to the stagecoach road. Keeping in the deeper roadside shadows, the dwarf struggled on to the great shadowed arch where the stagecoach road joined the tavern driveway.

There, in a dim filtering of moonlight, directly beside the trap he had so carefully devised and set, Amos saw two sprawled bodies. Sylvia and Robin lay together in death, their lifeblood poured over the brave new grass.

Amos stumbled toward them, then sank to his stubby knees, the burden of centuries weighing on him. Earth, earth had taken them. . . . Earth would take him. Mothering earth, soft and comforting, like Sylvia's dead breasts.

There was no cemetery in the Kessler countryside. The tavern lacked the precedence and luxury of a family graveyard. So, next day, Amos and his mother buried the lovers there in the forest near the roadside. And between the oak tree and the locust, Amos planted a rambler rose. In due time it blossomed red, almost blood red.

MATTER OF CHOICE

In the Ozarks, as elsewhere, there are seeming slow wits who keep on emerging as quick wits. Here is such a story, a tellin' story which is hardly more than an anecdote. My own belief is that it tells more than it says. Its conflict and motivation are rooted in one of the more profound realms of man's passion, his timeless affection for his animal possessions. In this and other responses Tobe Popper, like most rural Ozarkers and certainly like those the writer has known, was a sentient being in an environment where sensation and feeling predominate. On that basis Tobe Popper liked women, but he liked hawgs better. The related tellin' story is grounded in the Ozarker's gift for compassionate satire.

$\mathbb{S}$QUIRE Hunnicutt lit his pipe, scooted forward in his petticoated rocking chair, and turned toward his one and cherished daughter.

"Flory, I was a-thinkin'. I'm gettin' along in years. The farm is got to be kept up and goin'—livestock tended and all such as that. So I was thinkin' about you and that upcomin' Tobe Popper."

Flory Hunnicutt munched at a stick of candy lately presented by this same Tobe Popper, champion hog-raiser and young man of promise, and continued brier-stitching a birth-day handkerchief.

"Yes, Pa." She brier-stitched again, again, and again. "Well, Tobe is nice, and Summer Erp is nice, too. But Summer is a lot funnier," she pointed out with a subdued feminine slurp. "He can say funny things, and it's so mighty funny the way he can throw his voice—'Member the time he had Uncle Lige Martin's whiskers cheepin' like they was full of singin' catbirds? 'Member how up at the picnic Summer made a big boiled ham say to the schoolteacher, 'Treat me easy, sister! You already et four pounds!'?"

Squire Hunnicutt remembered. Summer Erp was close to the most comical young feller he had ever had around. But Flory's pappy likewise recollected that the Erp boy was about as worthless as they ever come. What was closer to the prac-tical reckonings, Squire Hunnicutt ran a hog farm, and since both Tobe Popper and Summer Erp were in a marrying frame of mind and both paying heed to his daughter Flory, the Squire favored Tobe Popper, admittedly the champion hog-raiser of Burnin' Bush Holler.

The Squire puffed and pondered. "Flory, how would it do for us to test out them boys and see for ourselves which one of 'em can bring up the tastiest pig, and also get some idea of their leanin's and inclinations—same time we're judgin' the hawgs. Let's tell 'em that the winnin' hawg will be killed and roasted for the big play-party up to the schoolhouse next week. The party's Friday night. We can do the judgin' Thurs-day aft'noon."

Flory brier-stitched her consent.

Thursday aft'noon came—Thursday aft'noons do. Tobe Popper spent the morning at useful work. Summer Erp, on the other hand, roamed among the wild gulches of Cheshire Hollow, enjoying nature and, incidentally, rounding up his pig Hybiscus, who was a lean and motley razorback—admittedly a scrub hawg from the wooded wilds. Summer called, "Pig—ooo——eee!" Finding that word and noise completely irresistible, Hybiscus trailed after his master up the long trail to the schoolhouse and possible destruction.

After an immense amount of thought, mostly deep, Tobe Popper picked from his model hog pen a plump, symmetrical, complacent, pinkish-white pig named Walter. That done, he hitched a rope just below the shank of Walter's left leg and headed him for the place of judgment. The rivals met among the hitching posts behind the schoolhouse. Tobe spoke first, with a smile that seemed a trifle fishy. "That there's a reemarkable hawg you brought, Summer! Must a took some mighty hard runnin' to ketch it!"

Summer Erp yawned and looked for a place to sit down. "Uh-huh, yours is a lot better pig than mine. He's got a nice shape. Nice eyes. Looks like a downright shame to kill such a nice hawg as that one, don't it, Tobe?"

Walter seemed to squeal softly, and Tobe Popper waited in uneasy silence. Summer Erp went on sleepily. "Your pig's dead for shore to win, too, Tobe, and I do mean dead for shore. . . . Reckon you and Flory will be mighty happy after you gits married up. But, you know, Tobe, when you and Flory gits married you'll be obliged to kill anyway twice as many hawgs every autumn as you got to now. . . ."

Tobe Popper squirmed but made no answer. Walter squealed wistfully, and Summer Erp continued. "Then after you've been married a spell—say, two, three years—it'll take likely four times as many hawgs. After two, three more years, it'll take five or six times as many hawgs. One good fat hawg for ever' member of the family . . . that there was what my pappy always said."

Having said that, Summer Erp dozed. Tobe Popper waited nervously. Then footsteps sounded from down the pathway. Squire Hunnicutt and his daughter Flory were arriving to judge the pigs. Squire Hunnicutt came straight to the business. He lit his pipe and scattered a pocketful of shelled corn. The two pigs ate side by side; Walter, tomorrow's touching excellence, versus Hybiscus, old-fashioned worthlessness. Summer Erp seemed to be asleep. Flory studied the prospects a little sadly.

"Looks like Tobe's brought the best pig. It's so friendly and fat and unsuspectin'."

"OOOOMMMMMP!" It *seemed* to be Walter who grunted. To Tobe Popper, an authority on pig grunts, this particular grunt told of abused friendship and trust.

"But Summer's pig—well, it's sort of *ex*-ceptional. Ain't in line of the usual, that is . . . ."

Just then Walter squealed again, so sorrowfully that Flory exclaimed, "It does look like Tobe's pig understands every word we say!"

Tobe Popper coughed and shifted his weight to his other foot. Squire Hunnicutt nodded judiciously and came straight to business. "They's only one way of votin' on them shoats. I vote for Tobe's!"

"Eeeeeeeeeekkkk, eek, eek, umpff, ummpff, umpfff." Again, it seemed to be Walter, filled to the brim with piteous grief—Walter, who was being chosen to be eaten.

"It just does look like that pig can understand *every word we say!*"

Again Squire Hunnicutt agreed with his daughter Flory. "Blamed if he don't!" Then noticing that Tobe Popper paced to and fro in tearing indecision, Squire Hunnicutt suggested, "Well, Tobe, I guess you'd best slaughter 'im right away."

"EEEEEEEEKKKKKK, eeek, eeek, umf, umf, umf, umf umf umf! *Eeeekkkkkk!*"

Walter's pleadings echoed far. Tobe Popper stepped into the open and braced himself against a hitching post. Then he cleared his throat and spoke brokenly, "I can't do it! I can't do it! So go ahead! Go 'head and leave Summer slaughter his pig and also take Flory. I just simply can't be ontrue to my hawg Walter."

Squire Hunnicutt ran a leather-brown hand through his graying hair. "Well, I'll be a pie-eyed heifer!"

For the moment Flory looked wonder-stricken, then slowly she smiled and clasped her hands and looked on the apparently slumbering Summer Erp. She smiled again and turned about like one awaking from a dream too beautiful to last.

Father and daughter turned away, down the pathway home. For a time Tobe Popper stroked his pig Walter's bristles. Then he went to wake Summer Erp. But rather oddly, Summer was already awake.

Tobe frowned. "Well, they come and judged, and all unbeknownst to you, I draws out and gives you the prize—that is, I give you Flory."

"I just do know!"

Tobe Popper stepped closer. "Now, looky here, you punkin-rollin' clodhopper! Can't you see what I done for you—sacrificin' all my likin's and e-fections for Flory and allowin' that bonestack of an acorn-fed razerback runt to win over a real handsome, breed-benefittin', upright hawg, such as Walter!"

Summer Erp mused. "I'm obliged to you, Tobe, I'm much obliged."

Tobe Popper rehitched the rope about Walter's shank and spoke more gently, "Well, you sleep-pretendin', voice-throwin' hoss thief and hawg faker, I hope you all, that is, you and Flory, will be gettin' along nicely."

"Thanks, Tobe."

"And understand, what I done wasn't done because I don't like women. I do. It's only that I like hawgs better."

MIRACLE CAVE

To speak frankly, this story puzzles me. I first heard it during the course of an extremely hot August afternoon near the foothill crossroads of Altus, Arkansas, back in 1926. I was nearing the end of a tramping trip down the engaging courses of the Mulberry rivers in the southwestern fringe of the Ozarks.

Presently a huge dark cloud bank began to show from the not-too-distant Oklahoma frontier. It was a welcome sight, but, in the manner of summer Ozarks storms, its approach was rife with fierceness. I looked about for a sheltered place and sighted a cluster of stone buildings. It was the monastery called Subiaco.

While waiting out the storm, I met a fat, stuttering friar dressed in ragged dungarees and the most dissolute straw hat I have ever seen off stage. The friar confided that he spent his days molding big bricks and dreaming small dreams. He added that he had been born and raised on Little Mulberry River and that he had first found the miracle of salvation in the many limestone caves near his birthplace and the remarkable birdlife in or near the shallower caves. When I urged him to tell more, he accommodated with a succession of rather painfully stammered vignettes that somehow built together into a most unusual tellin' story. After the rainstorm abated, the friar noted that he owed God a period of special prayers of thanksgiving for the rain.

After he had waddled from sight, I went my own way. The following summer when I called again at Subiaco, they told me that the brother had very recently departed for Paradise.

THE onetime settlement called Ginger Blue was never molested by through roads. Its most direct approach was by way of a forest trail that skirted the lower foothills of Cato Mountain and led to the White Star branch of War Eagle River.

The Ginger Blue settlement slept along in the next bend of valley. Before Civil War times the Matthew family had homesteaded the west slope of the smaller hillside beyond the first cluster of valley homesteads. The Matthew sons, Abel and Alfred, lived on in their birthplace and their differences.

The differences had come about quite gradually. In their childhood the brothers, whose ages were only a little more than a year apart, looked more alike than many twins. But when they came into their teens, the brothers began to shed their likeness one to the other. Abel seemed to leap into prime; he quickly grew taller and handsomer than his brother and very much lighter of spirit.

Alfred, by contrast, did not grow taller. Instead his broad shoulders became more stooped. The passing years left him less gay, more silent and solitary. When he occasionally spoke, the younger brother spoke strangely and sometimes in parables. He told of what the waiting stars and the living leaves and the singing winds were speaking. More and more insistently Alfred lived unto himself and walked alone.

As he came to man's age, he grew even more solitary and more and more disposed to walk alone in the hills. This puzzled the older brother and whetted his curiosity. One day Abel set out to follow Alfred on one of his increasingly frequent all-day rambles.

With great caution and keeping closely in forested shadows, the older Matthew trailed his younger brother into the far reaches of Willow Valley where footpaths fade away into shoulder-high grass and dense fringes of thorn bush. After several miles of the wilderness invasion, the younger brother began picking his way through the boulder-strewn draw of a great ravine and presently disappeared into a blockade of bluffs.

Abel was certain that here was the entrance to a cave. All of the valley people had heard of Miracle Cave, but one gathers that few had actually entered it. For it was said that the cave was a place of unholy magic which had served earlier as refuge for a spell caster from far south in the voodoo country. Hill people agreed that the spell caster had long since gone his way but that his evil magic had stayed.

As Abel toiled toward the cave entrance, he saw directly before him a great black shadow. He hesitated as a huge low-flying bird whirred close to his head and circled into the lower ravine. An instant later a flock of giant crows flew above the trespasser and disappeared into the walled base of Cato Mountain.

Abel tried harder to locate the cave entrance. While he was trying to climb over a barricade of slippery quartz, he lost his footing and fell forward, striking his head on an outcropping of rock. When he regained consciousness, he found himself sprawled on a moss bank with his brother kneeling beside him, using wet moss to stanch his forehead wound.

The two waited until daybreak to undertake the journey home. On the way, when Abel thanked his brother for saving his life, Alfred replied that he thanked Abel for saving his soul.

Within the year Abel went forth from his homeland, and for more than twenty years he did not return. But Alfred stayed on in ever increasing loneliness with the open hills his only companions.

When Abel came back at last, he was as ragged and gray as his younger brother, with whom he once more walked forth into the hills. And as they walked, Abel felt the burden of his passing years. "I feel as old as these hills, and I have not found their contentment. I choose to go forth again and guide by a new star."

"Find patience, brother. You still have years of life."

"But I have lost the juice of it—my youth."

In heavy silence the two walked on, far down into the wilderness-crowded foothills until they came to the lost river, and beside it they stopped to rest. Dawn still colored the water, and the hills seemed softened, as if by the mists of a million dead years.

After a very long time the strange silence was broken by a loud cawing. Once more Abel saw dark shadows sweeping across the face of the river, and once more he saw directly overhead a great crowding flock of giant crows. Again the winged throng circled in the yellowing sunlight. With a great driving thrust the entire flock vanished into the cave entrance. Recalling his first encounter with Miracle Cave, Abel shivered as if he were suffering a cruel ague. "Those flying things are devils with wings and feathers," he said.

"You don't see their souls," Alfred replied. "You see only their ugly bodies."

"I could all but feel the evil of their eyes," the older brother said somberly.

"But the eyes of those crows are windows for miracles," the younger brother declared. "The prophet who once lived in yonder cave befriended those birds; in repayment they gave him their magic vision, unchanging and unblinded by the passing years—any number of them."

Alfred ceased speaking and pushed forward to within sight of the cave entrance. There the younger brother, who seemed so very old, knelt as if in prayer and presently prostrated himself in the fringing of forest grass. After a time he fell asleep.

Abel, meanwhile, waited alone in dour impatience. After he had made certain that his brother slept, with great care and stealth he began picking his way toward the much-impeded cave entrance.

When he came out again, Abel was quite certain that he heard his name called. He waited for a long time, hearing no other sound except his own breathing. Then, beyond the shadow of a doubt, he heard his name called again, his full name, and this time he was certain that the voice came from the entrance way to the cave. Once more Abel headed toward the bluff-fringed entrance way. Again he picked his way through the shoulder-high brambles and farther into the boulder-littered ravine that led to the cave entrance. Again he reached it; again he waited, silhouetted on the breast of the mountain, looking down on low-drifting clouds. Then once more he disappeared into the walled darkness.

From down the valley there sounded again the loud cawing of a sentinel crow. The younger of the Matthew brothers awakened, and when he had gotten uncertainly to his feet, he looked west toward the beginning sunset. And he saw then that his brother was beside him, his older brother, who was by then standing very straight and speaking with the voice of youth. As they again walked together into the lengthening shadows, Alfred noted that his brother walked like a very young man and that the wrinkles had faded from his face and his hair was no longer gray.

The two came into a stretch of valley which was still lighted with a final remnant of sunset, and there the younger brother, who was now so noticeably the older, paused to state with great reverence, "Beyond the sunset there are worlds yet unknown to age, where youth and springtime live on forever and a day. Beyond the sunset——"

Abel cut in unbelievingly, "I know what's beyond the sunset. It's everlasting night, the cold black night of death."

Alfred protested, "But we who have known a dawn can look ahead toward another dawn, and another, and another ——"

Abel laughed aloud. "I don't choose to keep forever looking ahead. I've made my choice—to bring back my lost morning, and, my poor old brother, I have won my choice."

"But only the calendar of God can truly turn ahead."

"You can believe that, you that can only grovel and beg with prayers. But I can see with eyes made young again, without the blur of moldy scriptures——"

Alfred cried out, "Only the true believer can find true resurrection of his youth."

A very dim pathway led through an abbey of forest elms, and there in the half-light the brother who had been the younger of the Matthews made out the shape of a grounded crow. The bird did not retreat but stumbled toward them, croaking. When Alfred looked closer, he saw that the huge crow was blind. Both of its eyes had been torn from their sockets, changing them into rounded bloody pits.

Abel stepped aside, laughed tauntingly, and, when the blinded bird groveled at his feet, he leaped to the top of a high outcropping of limestone and, holding high his right hand, shouted, "Be of good cheer, magic buzzard! I will give you back your eyes. But first I will use them to make a miracle of my own choosing! I will make the whole damned, foul, creaky, aging earth young again."

Alfred grasped at his brother's arm. But Abel moved nimbly beyond his reach. He opened his right hand, displaying two rounded and bluish gems that sparkled mightily in the failing light. The gems were colored like turquoise.

Facing the evening star, Abel called out, "All prophets,

hear this. These are the eyes of yon miracle bird. By their power I command. Now that I am young again, turn back all the world to match my own youngness!"

He had barely finished speaking when the dying sunset blazed forth again—a vast golden embankment of light. And to the east there arose a mighty half-circle of rainbows. And then there came a great deafening thunder of noise, coming closer and closer.

Alfred cried out, "My God, my God, this is the end of the world!"

When he turned toward his brother, Abel, he saw only a stooped gray monk fingering a crucifix.

RAIN

The dogging and in great part self-perpetuating poverty of the rural Ozarks is rooted in two very basic deficits, lack of adequately fertile soils and sufficiently dependable rainfall. The soil fertility is improvable. Here and there effective irrigation is attainable. But, as any Ozarker who has tried to live by his plow or hoe is well aware, successful irrigation is costly and inevitably dependent on available water sources and suitable topography. Withering drought is incorrigible and, in the Ozarks, recurring. By long-time averages two drought years in five can be expected. One in five is likely to be a "real scorcher."

One doesn't soon or easily forget the real scorchers. My last one on the scene was in 1952. By July of that year fruit trees and forest trees were dying at wholesale; vineyards were withering; corn stalks stood like twisted spears, and dying vegetable gardens were being further ravaged by great wind-blown swarms of grasshoppers and mass invasions of alien chewing and sucking insects. I remember spending the Fourth of July that year digging my drought-robbed potato crop from the hot dust while an undersized lizard, panting mightily, looked on. When I had finished excavating the ludicrously dwarfed potatoes, I dug out the remnants of withered root vegetables, chopped down the dying tomato plants, and then sought water for my thirsting cattle. Even the rivers were drying up.

All this is of the drying dregs of Ozarks living. The same holds for the following tellin' story. Elijah Shrum had lived through many crop-ruining, hope-blackening droughts, but this time he was losing something much more important than a crop.

I T was late July, the lathering, sweat-dripping dog days of an Ozarks summer, a time of animal-torturing heat and plant-twisting drought. Heat waves climbed from the failing pasture lands. Valley fields drooped and groveled as if to beg for rain. Afternoon shadows waited on bended knees, joining in the supplication. Even in the creekside plantings the corn stalks were twisted, and their tassels were drooping.

Elijah Shrum sat in the shade of a dwarf oak tree, whittling a stick of dead cedar wood, slicing it rather precisely into thin, vaguely pinkish slivers—wholly without usefulness. Momentarily the graying man reflected on the futility of his enterprise. In the beginning, Lije Shrum had set out to whittle a ninepin potato masher for his wife. He had taken up the chunk of cedar limb with that aim in mind. But stroke after stroke his pocket knife had shown up the faults of the wood. Now, after an hour, he had sliced away the punkwood until the stick was no longer anywhere thick enough to make a potato masher. He could have changed objectives, providing the foreblade of the pocketknife still had the strength to scoop out the head of a spoon. But Lije rather doubted that the metal was stout enough. Those red cedar knots do get wicked hard.

By the time he had recrossed his knees and tilted the split-bottom chair against the tree trunk at precisely the right angle for comfort, the stick of cedar was dwindled almost to finger size, too piddling small even to shave into a salting spoon. Life is like that, too.

While the whittler paused to nibble a half-twist of home-grown chewing tobacco he caught a sure look at a flicker bird—some call it a rain crow—that he had earlier heard.

Even the bird moved as if suffering from a heat stroke. It zigged to a maple tree top, then zagged down almost to the porch eaves, then flipped itself to the roof ridge of the Shrum cabin. There it sat, swaying slightly with lolling beak and drooping wings.

The old man laid aside his whittling, eased down the fore pegs of his straight chair, and began to peer about for a throwing rock. But the move was unfortunate. The flicker straightened itself, trotted somewhat blearily to the far side of the roof, raised its head, lifted its wings undecidedly, and called out. The odd lapse into unmusical sound ended in a kind of gasping tremulo. Then after a rather ridiculous flapping the bird took off again, headed for the tall oaks.

Lije was disturbed. He had always understood it is bad luck to have a flicker bird squawking from one's rooftop. It foretells a serious loss. Lije was an old man with pitiful little left to lose. About all he had left were his failing self, his old woman, their son, two rather sickly pigs, and a twelve-acre patch of corn that would most probably turn out nothing but a mess of squirrel headed nubbins that all hell couldn't shuck. His son also had a smidgen of a field. But the bodacious, hot, dry weather had it pretty well raped, too. Even so, this pesty bird had whooped from his rooftop.

Lije decided he would not continue with the meditation. Whatever was to be would be; so he went on with his whittling. Quite soon he stopped again. Too much sitting was cramping his leg muscles. Moreover, every time he breathed, the chair rounds appeared to squeak. That, too, was getting to be annoying. He put his knife back in his right side pocket, threw away the whittling stick, slid down from his chair, and lay at full length on the drying grass where the shade was deepest. It was far from being comfortable. But his mood was one of making do. He slid his hat over his eyes, rested his head on his sweated arm, and, for a time, dozed. Rags, dead years, drought-parched crops. But anyway, at least for a cat nap here and there, he could sleep.

Lije awoke with a feeling of cramped annoyance. Can't a man ever be left in peace? Where was that squeaking coming from? On it came, spreading out through the barnyard, high-pitched, blind of tune, annoying of rhythm. He sat upright. So it was Ma rolling the wheelbarrow. She had been digging the smattering of potatoes—getting them out of the ground before the sun cooked them where they grew. Damn pesty work, too, this digging potatoes in late July when the ground is dry as canned snuff and grown up in ragweeds shoulder high. But Ma had been saying that if only it would come a snatch of rain she could plant the patch to late sweet turnips. A foolish hope; Weeping Jesus Himself couldn't grow so much as a hill of beans in such weather.

The old woman set down the wheelbarrow and lifted out a basket partly filled with potatoes, few bigger than hen eggs, most barely marble-sized. Her dress flapped in the breeze. Sunlight played across the folds of faded apron. Her midparts had sweated her clothes tightly to her lean flesh. Her forearms were almost beet-red with sunburn.

"Purty hot out'n the sun?"

The old woman slipped to the grass in a posture of worn resignation. "Sizzlin', but I don't mind the heat like I do the everlastin' longness. Seems like these old summer days stretch forever."

"They'll end, all right." Lije was easily reassuring. Then he peered toward the east. "What you suppose that is up Fingers' lane?"

"Reckon hit's Sonny bringin' his nag down through the sumacs. Through with his plowin', I expect." The old woman peeled up the crown of her sunbonnet and stepped closer into the shadows. "I never see a lad so take to his crops. Considerin' his pa, I jest say hit's a livin' miracle."

Lije felt the sting of her words, but declined to reply in kind. He merely inquired, "What good will hit do him? That's what I'd like to know. Another few days of this heated dryness and they won't be enough corn in the whole holler to winter a red rooster, much less a coon."

There was a silence of gritty sultriness. When Ma turned, her forehead wrinkles seemed to deepen automatically. She glanced at the red upsides of her sunburned hands. "Yeah. Well, Sonny figgers that if he can make a corn crop he can sell it off for enough to learn to be a auto mee-chanic with. He allows that's what he wants to be. Been talkin' about it for most of a year. Says he can take the schoolin' and go down to Fort Smith and make four dollars a day cash money tinkerin' and mendin' autymobiles."

"That don't make no sense. Even them sinful money handlers in them big bank houses don't git that kind of money. Besides, they jest ain't enough autos to keep him putterin' steady——"

"Maybe you don't know, Lige Shrum. Could be for maybe the once you jest don't know."

"Well anyhow, if he's figgerin' to have his corn crop for to send him out and learn him to be a auto mee-chanic, he shore ain't goin' nowhere. They ain't goin' to be no corn crop. Give another week of this burn-up dryin' weather . . . give two, three more days . . ."

"What you perticklar keep harpin' on that for?"

"No certain, setup reason, I guess. It's only——"

His old woman pulled a blade of yellow grass and chewed on it broodingly. The jingling sounds were coming closer. There was Sonny now, slipping the plow harness off the sweat-streaked sorrel. He grinned at his father. "Awful hot day." But his tone was not one of protest or lament.

Lije nodded judiciously. "How'd you make it with the plowin'?"

"Finished it. Finished layin' off. Counted off forty-nine furrows since dinnertime. I'm jest about sweated down to a streak of salt."

"Where's the hoss goin'?"

"Yonderways to sedge grass. He jest now took out. Like maybe you can hear, I put the bell on the ole bastard so as he won't be too hard to track down."

There was a swishing of sweat-wet denim and a snatch of a newfangled tune as Sonny strolled to the back porch. Lije settled back to his resting. "This here's the decidin' week for the corn crop. Hit's comin' into tassels right now. . . . No rain, no ears." He paused for emphasis.

The old woman peered at him closely. "Why you keep on harpin'?"

Lije frowned. "Last night I see the moon was dry. Moon's put there to tell the seasons and weather——"

The old woman's expression was one of great weariness. "I ain't fixed too certain of that there. I'd kind of feel for rain."

The shade was thinning. The latening sunlight seemed sulfurous yellow and flesh searing. Lije noted a grim, gray catbird perched in the almost leafless lilac bush. He could figure no particular meaning to that. But his shaded resting place was no longer shaded. The tree shadows seemed thin as wagon spokes. Begrudgingly he carried his squeaking chair to the front porch. Through the hot little tunnel of a hallway he could see the sunset now—a fiery ball sinking into a valley dimmed by a bluish haze. The sunset was turning deep yellow. A rain sign, for sure. Lije rammed his hands into his breeches pockets. If a good big rain should come, Sonny's corn patch would probably make a crop; it was the only new ground on the place. Sonny would sell the corn and be taking off. Lije found himself feeling strangely tired. He strolled to the washstand, took down the tin dipper and lifted himself a drink of water. It was warm as fresh blood. He poured the water back into the bucket and replaced the dipper.

Supper was a quarter-hour of comparative silence with milk mush, cornbread and honey, an almost colorless chunk of salt pork, and the leftovers from a blackberry cobbler. Sonny was hungry, as boys will be, but he finished hurriedly, topped his bowl with knife and fork, and left the table. He said he had something to tinker about in the loft. That was what he said. Lije knew that Sonny was going for a prowl in the moonlight. His wife cleared away the dimly purple remnant of her cobbler, propped her elbows on the table. "Had a-plenty?"

Lije nodded. "Wouldn't care for nothin' more. I ain't real hongry."

The old woman motioned aimlessly toward the door. "Hear that rain crow hollerin' this soon after sundown?"

"Uh-huh."

"Old Man Fiety done put his boys to haulin' in their hay crop."

Rain, rain, rain. Lije rose heavily. Rain, and the corn crop would be got made, and there he would be with nobody to see about but his old woman! Creeping, weeping Jesus!

"Guess it wasn't no great job for them Fietys. All the hay they scythed would fill a box wagon."

Fireflies were floating forth from the blackening cavalcade of the night, darting here and there, flashing their lights with an odd restlessness. Though he did not comment, Lije understood. The fireflies also had the feel of rain.

He strolled down to the front gate, very deliberately propped his elbows on the big post, took a homemade clay pipe from his left-hand breeches pocket, crammed its bowl with brittle leaf tobacco, struck a match, and puffed very hard. After a begrudging salute of smoke arose, Lije took the pipestem from his teeth and tapped his right foot in the dust. Dust of the dead years. But even the looks of the dust had changed. He turned back to the cabin. A tree frog called from a grove of valley sycamores far down beside Skull Branch. First tree frog Lije had heard in a month. And when a tree frog prays for rain, the Lord listens. Dim moonlight touched the treetops. Lije looked up into the top branches of nearby trees. Even in first moonlight the oak leaves looked oddly tousled. Still another sign of rain.

Lije retreated to the porch, took a chair, and propped it against the cedar-column post. He heard Sonny strolling through the house. Next, from a far valley, he heard a murmur like the song of a far-off ocean. An oncoming storm can put the hills to talking. The old woman was inside, flouncing about on the bed. Could it be an oncoming change of weather was bringing on a spell of her damnable rheumatism? Lije rose and pushed aside his chair and walked out into the night. For a time he sprawled again on the grass, which felt oddly cool. Chances for a snatch of rest seemed better outdoors than indoors.

Lije awoke quite abruptly. Night wind swooped down on him and went away into the big woods on Newcomb's Mountain. To the northwest he saw a blue fantasy of lightning. A whitish fluffery of clouds had curtained away the moonlight.

An old-time northwester summer rainstorm!

Lije got to his feet, felt himself staggery before the might of the arriving storm. Then he heard the bellow of thunder. A big raindrop struck his cheek. There would be many of them soon—sheets, acres, blockades, and torrents of raindrops. Fattening rain, greedy rain, pillaging rain. Rain that would wash away the last of his daydreams. Rain that would take away his boy.

Vast tongues of lightning darted toward the higher arches of sky. There was a succession of splintering roars. That opened the big bucket. Lije brushed the hair from his eyes and crowded close against the biggest of the yardway oaks. For a moment he only heard the great battering of raindrops on its big leaves. Then he saw first miniature rivulets run down the crevices in the tree's bark; then he felt a great drenching mist breaking through the extremely temporary barrier of leaves.

Stooping low, Lije trotted toward the protecting porch. To his astonishment he stumbled against the steps, saw abrupt blurs of bronze and purple. He smelled a strange aroma of sulfur and newly mown grass—the lightning was damn sure striking close by. Ma and Sonny were standing before him, tousled and strange. Sonny was on tiptoe, and he was calling out, "Rain! How ye like it, Pa? Rain!" He was jubilant. "Can't you just hear them corn stalks laughin'? They're only gigglin' now, but comes mebbe five minutes more they'll be right out hawhawin'. Corn? This here'll fill out the ears and fill up wagons. Don't care if it don't rain another drap; we'll git corn. I can sell mine, the whole patch standin'—now—tomorry mornin', to Seff Connell. Bet he'll mebbe pay twenty dollars cash down for like hit stands now. Seff's a-buyin' corn for Van Winkle and Dickie Saunders. They're feedin' hawgs and brewin' licker. I'm ready on my way to Fort Smith and mechanickin'!"

Lije felt an overwhelming craving to pull his son to him, to hold him in an unbreakable embrace—forever and ever. It was an old man's folly, nothing but old man's folly! He might as well go tucking in to bed. The rain had him beat down for sure and final. The best he could do, damn near all he could do now, was to get in some snoozing. Why? Best ask, why not?

MARTHY COMES HOME

In the Ozarks, as elsewhere, people come and go and, sometimes, come again. Intermittently incomings or outgoings have predominated, but for the most part they have been more in the manner of changeable trickles than steadfast tides. On that basis, particularly during the past fifty years, the exoduses have been most markedly from the rural villages and the farther backwoods. For the most part the larger towns have scored the principal gains, the farther back counties the most impressive losses. Whatever the specific motivations, which are usually climatic and economic, odds are at least twenty-to-one that Ozarkers who leave will not come back.

This, too, has been going on for a long time. One recurring testimony consists of the county seats which, as communities, are now dwindling or almost completely nonexistent. The supporting evidence includes the sometimes grass-grown meandering of what once were the stage roads or the farm roads that now have gone back to bush and sedge grass because the farms and farming communities they once served have passed away. Alongside the deceased roads one finds cellar holes, persisting rows of daffodils or other long-lived bulb plants, or one-time shade trees or yardway shrubs that have survived the prolonged encroachment of tall weeds and short underbrush.

There is consolation and a degree of redemption in the wonderful talent of Ozarks lands to live on without people, to perpetuate great beauty without mortal onlookers.

In their slow and oftentimes entangled, stubbornly distinctive ways the chronicles of Ozarks people who go out or come in provide highly effective tellin' stories. These stories tend to possess a strange and winsome charm and a profound depth of sincere and lucid compassion.

A glass of drinkin' water? Why shorely! Mebbe you'd care to come and set a spell. That's what rockin' chairs is for—to yield rest to them that is tired out of walkin'. Like I used to say to Marthy—she was my sister—she still is my sister. Anyway, when me and Marthy was gabbin' about how we might get Uncle Billy Rutherford to bottom them chairs that Grandpa Rudolph trailed overland from Alabamy back in the 1840's, I says, "Marthy, it ain't just for ourselves that we ought to have more chairs about; it's for other folks that will be droppin' by tired and needin' to set down worse'n me and you."

But here I am commencin' to talk while leavin' you settin' there to thirst. Like my Pa used to say to me, "Myrtle," he'd say, "if you'd work as much as you talk you'd shore be a wheelhoss for labor." Pa was everlastin' naggin' after me for not gettin' to the point. Reckon I sort of lean to Ma's ways; she was always right smart of a talker and allowed there wasn't much point to makin' points. I took after my Ma in most every way, but Marthy, she was always more like our Pa.

I reckon I'm bound to keep on talkin' about Marthy today. You see—but wait just a minute while I go and fetch a pitcher of cool milk. Just set a minute——

Well, here we be, milk enough for two or three dipperfuls and two cuts of cake, seein' as how you're a man. Like Marthy used to say about men—even before she first went to teethin'

Marthy always did like men. And it do seem like today I can't talk about nobody but Marthy, on account of today's her time for homecomin', and I ain't saw her, not once, for nine years last corn-plantin'. That's a right long time not to see a body's sister, perticular when that sister is all I got left.

And this here's the day Marthy's comin' home, and when I first heard you come brushin' through them laneside leaves, for a minute I thought I'd plum choke. Of course when you come closer I knowed the steps was them of a man. But what I set out to say was that me and my sister Marthy is all they's left of the Carney folks that settled all this here holler and the left-hand fork of Deerbone Branch. Me and Marthy was borned and raised right here in this old shack where my Pa was borned and died. Us two growed up together here. And after Ma died, that was when Marthy was teethin', me bein' the oldest, my Pa allowed as I had ought to look after the youngest one.

So I done most of the raisin' of Marthy, and since first I can recollect I reckoned in private that the sun rose and set in her. I built her playhouses and pretty moss banks along the creek bed. I made her hemstitching, also gingerbread cookies. When she was commencin' to learn to talk, we'd gabble baby talk together, and Pa he says, "Law goodness sakes, that young'un can't never learn to talk if you keep on that jabberin' at her in baby talk, so shet it up." Then Pa used to say when Marthy would go to sleep on my lap at night, he'd say, "God's sake, that child can't never grow up womanlike being forever babied like you do with her." But I reckon Pa was wrong about that, because she did grow up, the same as everbody else does, and she come out a woman.

And when Pa died—that was after Marthy was well growed—it left us sort of stranded as you could put it. I didn't too much mind; I never owned but mighty little, I never wanted but mighty little, and I never minded being off by myself, anyhow, as long as Marthy was here.

Marthy, she is different. You see, she's emeralds and di'monds and jasmines, whilst I'm only oat heads or maybe corn tawsles. Two winters me and her went to school, back when Matt Morry started his academy school down on Hazel Creek, and Marthy, she jest simply loved and cherished it plum to death. Seems like it opened up new worlds and places for her—far off and wonderlike.

They haven't been no great number of folks comin' in these parts for a good many years. One foreigner did come about fourteen years ago. He give his name as John Starr, which didn't strike me as bein' much of a name. Anyway, his name was said to be John Starr, and, while I don't know a lot about men and he wasn't no great shakes young, the first time I see him I says to Marthy, "Marthy, that there's a not too mighty likely man."

Marthy appeared like she already knowed it. . . . Let's raise a window, so we can fetch in the cool air—ummm, smell them wild grape blossoms. . . . So, anyhow, I'd commenced to tell you about John Starr. Well, the first time I even seen him, he come a-strollin' up that pathway there about the same way as you did. He took off his hat, and I seen he was honest sun-browned and that his hair was gray-streaked and his eyes cleanlike, and, when he smiled, I seen he had good sound teeth.

He says, "I come to ask could I tote home some drinkin' water out'n your well." Then he stopped for to chat. Told me he was homesteadin' down on Miser's Fork. Said he'd built a log shack to live in, but didn't have nothin' else, and he reckoned he'd have a fling at sheep raisin'. I asked him was that his line, and he grinned and says his line was everwhere there was forest and mountains and land for the free takin'. Said he'd herded sheep and rode cattle range and sailored on boats and chopped timber and worked saw rigs and done a bit of most everthing. Said he'd worked far north and far south and east and far west and done lots of things in all sorts of places and then some.

After a spell Marthy come in from the old smokehouse. They spoke howdy, both of 'em shy, and Marthy whispers out to me that as she stepped into that smokehouse, a great big rat come makin' straight at her. Marthy never could stand the sight of rats.

The man speaks up like as if she'd spoke it all out loud. "Where's your smokehouse at? I got some mighty fine medicine for rats," he says. Marthy told him, and he strolled up toward it and pulled open the door, then stepped back and smacked a rock against the side of the shack.

When he done that, out come that huge big rat, scurryin' off down the backyard path. Well, John Starr stood stark still a second or so; then, all at a flash, he reached into his pocket and pulled out a pistol gun, all shiny with oil, and leveled it down and pulled the trigger and banged away. That big rat plunged into the air, turned a somersault, and flopped down as dead as Adam. So whatever's his real name jest put his pistol gun back into his pants pocket and went to drawin' his water.

He come for drinkin' water now and then for the best part of a month, only stoppin' for to speak howdy. Then come a night late in August when he come to the house and said he'd just finished diggin' a well of his own and wouldn't need to carry no more drinkin' water and thanked us kindly.

He said it was no fun to tote drinkin' water for two miles and a half but that good company had more'n made up for the trampin'. Marthy sort of flushed at that, but Johnny just kept on talkin' about this and that, mainly about the ewes he'd brought from over at West Fork to graze on his flint pasture.

Then all at once he says, "You know this here is late August, and next month they're havin' the county fair up to Fayettsvul'." He says he allowed he'd go, bein' as how he'd late bought hisself a wagon and a span of mules, and he said he'd shore be mighty pleased if Marthy and me would honor him with drivin' in to the fair next Tuesday week. I seen Marthy wanted to go real bad, so I said I'd go all right, and Marthy says she was mightily obliged and would be real happy to go.

So we all three took in that fair. John Starr come drivin' up in a new spring wagon and with about the best-lookin' span of mules you ever seen, and he was fresh shaved and lookin' right handsome. We climbed in the seat, and it was a nice trip. I kept thinkin' it would rain every minute, but it didn't. Finally we come to the fairgrounds, and John drove in and tossed three silver half-dollars to the gatekeeper without once budgin'. Then, after he had unhitched the hosses and put 'em to eatin' hay in the shade, we went to look at the ex-ibits. An' it was a fine fair an' a fine day. After we'd looked a spell we strolled over and et catfish sandwiches and drank lemonade. Then John said did we want to ride on the merry-go-round, and Marthy acted like she might like it, only I said it would look mighty silly for folks our age. I sort of wished I hadn't of said that, on account of Marthy looked so young and nice. She was wearin' her butterfly-yeller dress, and she was true beautiful in it. Her shoes was all polished up, and she had on a glass bead necklace that Pa brought back the time he went to the glass factory down to Van Buren when she was nine.

So then we went back to see the rest of the ex-ibits, and, as we went through the stalls, we seen some of the purtiest cow-beasts and layin' hens and ducks and geese and hawgs and goats I ever see anywhere. When we come to the sheep, we stopped up in front of a ram that was all washed and glistenin' white and slick, and Johnny Starr laughs and says, "Guess whose that'n is?" So I looked at the name card, and I seen it belonged to him. When Marthy and me says what a nice sheep it is, he looked pleased like a little boy that's been bragged about.

Then we went through the ex-ibits of canned goods, and they was nice enough but no better'n me and Marthy done. Directly then we went out to look at the race horses, but Johnny says they was kinda porely, and he sure spoke like as how he knew what he was talkin' about. After that he led us around to the shootin' stall, and that's where we come mighty close to havin' trouble.

Some fellers there had cat rifles and rows of clay targets. You'd pay a dime and go up to the board shelf and stand there and shoot at the targets that moved back and forth in front of a line of bags—they was shaped to look like flyin' ducks and swimmin' fish and what-not—and whoever had the cat rifle would shoot, and there wasn't no doubt about it if he hit, because the targets would bust into umsteen pieces. The way it worked, you'd pay a dime to shoot three times, and if you hit twice you'd get the dime back and three times you'd git a quarter back. We stood around awhile and watched folks shoot, and it appeared like nobody was hittin' much. Well John Starr and Marthy edged up closer, and directly the feller that was at the stall seen Johnny and held out a cat rifle, all bright and shiny, and says, "Better have a round, Mister—it only costs a dime."

Johnny said he'd have a try. So he took up the rifle and felt of it; then raised it to his shoulder and banged away three times and didn't hit nothin'. Everybody around commenced to grin and fidget, and the stallkeeper says, "Better try again!"

and Marthy looked like she'd plum sink into the ground. Johnny commenced to shoot again. That time the li'l rifle went rat-tat-tat like a woodpecker at work on a cedar fence post, and three of them targets busted all to smithereens. There wasn't nobody grinnin' after that; that is, nobody but Marthy. So then the stallkeeper shelled out a bright shiny quarter kind of uneasy like, but Johnny shoved it back and says, "Keep it, son. Hit'll help you to buy new targets, because by time I get done here you'll be needin' a whole tubful of 'em!"

And he did, too. Because Johnny Starr busted about a dozen more shootin' from the right shoulder. Then he switched the gun over to his left shoulder and busted up another lot. Then he commenced shootin' from low down on his side and kept right on bustin' them clay gismoes jist the same. And you know, that man kept shootin' till there wasn't a single target left nowhere about that stand. And when he turned away, why nearly everybody on the whole fairgrounds was standin' to watch. Then Johnny handed the feller back his rifle and flipped him a new shiny dollar.

"There you be, sonny," he says. "And the reason I busted up your show was because this here's a crooked weapon. The sights of this cat rifle is so lined that anybody who didn't know better would be shootin' high all day long."

The feller taken the gun back and didn't say a word, not one word. And when Johnny turned around a tall man with a big silver star steps up—that was Lem Guinn, he was sheriff —he steps up and says, "Looks like you know considerable about gunnery, Mister!"

John Starr eased back and says, "Used to be I did, but these cat rifles don't mean too much!"

The sheriff was eyein' him mighty close. "I don't believe I got your name," he says.

"John Starr."

"Are you shore?" the sheriff asks.

Johnny drawed himself up tall and straight and says, "I'm shore. I'm livin' down about seven miles past West Fork, and if I can help you, call on me!" With that he motioned to me and Marthy, and so we walked off, but we finished over-lookin' the fair and didn't get home till long after dark. But first he blowed us to supper at Gholson's restaurant in Fayetts-vul, and when we finally got home he handed to Marthy all the plunder he'd been pickin' up all day—cotton candy and peanuts and squeakers and popcorn and pamphlets about squab raisin' and mixin' mortar and raisin' Belgian hares, and cards with pictures of houses burnin' down when you looked at 'em through red celluloid, and a bushelful more things and stuff. So I told Johnny "Whoever" I was powerful obliged and didn't recollect when we had had so much of good plea-surables, which was right, and went on in the house. Well, Marthy set there on the dashboard and talked a long spell, and when she finally come in, it was truly late.

Well, that night was the last I ever see of Johnny Starr. Next day was Friday, and Marthy and me washed; I done most of it because Marthy was walkin' around in a fuzzy, gold-dusty daze, daydreamin' like she done when she was a real young girl. All day long she didn't say scarcely nothin'. But I knowed she'd fell for sure and all over in love with the one called Johnny Starr. I knowed for sure that if she went off with him I'd just about die. Still and all, I didn't blame her none. Like I say, Marthy always was the man-likin' kind.

But nothin' more happened, at least not right away. Like always, me and Marthy opened the fall work, startin' with kraut settin', makin' apple butter, then scythin' the late hay and workin' the sorghum molasses. Then come corn gatherin' and hog killin', and yet another winter was set in.

All this time Marthy was considerable moody and, like as not, spleeny. Things about the farm appeared to rub her cross-ways. Like one mornin' whilst we was out cookin' up hawg cracklin's and makin' soap, she bobs up to me and says, "All this here is nasty and ugly. It makes me sick like to die of." Then she throws her hands up and went plungin' into the house and flops down on her bed and cried like I hadn't see her do in half a lifetime.

Then one day come the tail end of November, Marthy just up and walked all the way into Fayetts-vul—fourteen miles off—roused out before sunup and didn't come home till I was at washin' the night dishes and creamers. She didn't say nothin' about what she'd went for, and I didn't see nothin' she brought back except a bottle of ink and a writin' pen and envelopes and a tablet.

After that, she done a sight of letter writin', mostly late of night, sometimes settin' there in the lamplight, scratchin' away like settled in a dream. Well, that went on, off and on for months, and I was considerably puzzled, because she didn't never have any of them postal stamps that's got to go on mailed letters and I was thoughty sure she was bound to be gettin' letters, too.

Come February it was, I set at doin' some quiltin'. One mornin' I was around lookin' for old dresses and everwhat would be handy to scrap up, and I come across the ditty box that Marthy used to keep her play-purties in when she was a little girl child. Whenever I moved that box the lid come bulgin' off, and I seen that the top was all fat and filled up with letters. Well, I read one of 'em. I ought not to a done it, but Marthy was out piddlin' about the woodlot, and I was female curious.

The letters was wrote by John Starr, like I figgered, and none of 'em had stamps on 'em. The letter I read commenced with Johnny sayin' he hadn't been outside none because he had misery in his legs and shoulders. He said he didn't have nothin' much to eat except stewed mutton and hawg meat and cornbread, and that didn't seem to do him no good. Said he hadn't been to Fayetts-vul no more because it seemed like folks there suspicioned him. He went on like that for a space, then finally he says he truly loved Marthy, and everwhen she needed a home to come to, why he'd be at his'n waitin' for her.

That was all that topmost letter said, but I had the feelin' that pretty soon Marthy would be takin' off again, she bein' a natural woman and that bein' a natural woman's way. One day about a week afterwards, Marthy spent a whole day cookin' and set out two lard buckets filled up with victuals, without sayin' nothin' about where or what for she was goin'. She didn't truly have to, on account it stood out like a washin' hung out on Sunday.

So March tromped through and turned April about the time the oak leaves gets to the size of a mouse's ear. About this time a girl child come up to the house one day, says her name was Snowbelle Appleby and she was a niece child of Leander Morry about midway 'tween here and Brushy Fork. She strolls up to me and says, "Aunt Philly"—that's Mrs. Morry —"sent me to bring this letter to Miz Carney. Be you Miz Carney?" So I says I be, and where was the letter?

"It's from the sheep rancher from down on Brushy Fork," she says. "Aunt Philly says you all have been leavin' letters at her house for each other since last fall, and she says I'd better bring this here one up because she and Uncle Leander is goin' home with me tomorry to visit my folks, and you'd be findin' the house locked up and couldn't redeem no such letters."

I see the whole thing. Marthy and John Starr had been writin' letters to each other and leavin' 'em at the Morry place.

The letter that little Snowbelle brung to me was for Marthy, but the child, not knowin' no better, had handed it to me 'cause I'm Miz Carney, too, same as Marthy be. So I thanked her kindly and give her some milk and cake, and laid the letter on the mantelpiece, and went back to work.

After while Marthy come in and took the letter without sayin' so much as one word.

Well, the next I hear tell about Johnny Starr was when I went in to Aumick's Store at Fayetts-vul to buy lamp chimneys and snuff for hen nests. And while I was standin' there chattin', I hear some folks from over about Miser Fork sayin' it looked ike there'd been some sheep stealin' goin' on over in their parts. Another party spoke out that they'd been losin' some grazin' cattle.

Uncle Dick Sanders, he's an old gent that don't do much but loaf around the stores, says, "You're sure it wasn't wolfs?" The first one says he never seen no wolfs wearin' saddle boots and drivin' livestock down a main road. I knowed they was talkin' about that John Starr. "He's a gunman from out West," one of 'em says. I didn't surely believe that, only I wasn't certain. Anyhow, I figgered John Starr or whatever he be could take care of hisself in case of trouble. But for sure I felt deep sorry for Marthy; I seen that whichever trouble happened to Johnny would fall a sight harder on her.

Come next day, Marthy and me commenced spring house-cleanin'. We lit in early and bustled along real brisk. When afternoon come we set to scrubbin' the floors. First I'd sweeped 'em with a new broom I'd only lately store-bought. I do scrubbin' with a old broom that's already wore down to a stub. Marthy fetched in a bucket of suds water and pitched in to scrubbin' with my brand new broom. That misrubbed me, so I says, "Marthy, you jist put that new broom up; we'll take turns at scrubbin' with the old one."

That there was the wrong thing to say; lookin' back, I see hit was. All at once Marthy went stanchy pale, slammed down the broom, and went stalkin' out. About a minute later she came back with her hat on and her old plunder box propped up under her arm. She was still pale, like the back side of a flour bag, and her mouth was set funny close.

"I'm leavin'," she says. "I got full up of bein' bossed and shooed around all my life like a teethin' toddler. I'm tired of it all, tired of stayin' all my life in this same old jail. I'm wore-out and tired of it all!"

For a minute I was considerable riled up, but then I commenced to feel sick-sorry for Marthy. She was cryin', but not like no young girl cries, on account of all at once my sister had commenced to look like a old lady. "I'm goin' to Johnny Starr's. I'm goin' right now," she says to me.

Marthy strode to the door lookin' straight before her. After she'd stepped down off the porch she turned about and says, "Goodbye." I wanted to hold her close in my arms like I used to when she was toddlin' young, but I knowed I couldn't do that no more. What I most wanted to do was to cry, too, but I was all dry inside like a corn nubbin' after a long summer drought. All what I said was, "Marthy, if you ever need a home again, I'll be here waitin'."

She got her light valise set and went pattin' off afoot; by then it was latenin' afternoon. I went back to the house because to watch a person out of sight means they're liable not ever to come back again. All next day and next week I felt heavy and choked up, like I'd been so many years ago when Marthy's pet sow littered pigs and they all died, and I had to slip out and bury them unbeknownst to her.

But the days kept on comin', and another springtime rolled in, and I took to tendin' the place again—plantin' out a garden, layin' off a cornpatch, and now and then cookin' a snack to eat. It ain't too hard takin' a livin' out of the ground jest for a body's self. Besides, like Pa used to say, I was borned simple. Marthy never was that way, which is rightful, on account of if it wasn't for her kind I reckon the rest of peoples would after while get like razorback hawgs.

Anyway, that first year after she took off I acted wicked lazylike. The crops mostly growed up to weeds. Even the garden went to naught. Expect I'd of about starved out that winter if it hadn't been for our milk cow and a cellarful of old cannin's and dryin's. But I come through it, and after that grievin' year I've held along purty good. Of course, it ain't near the same without Marthy. But I've got along. And it don't really seem like no nine years since she went off.

But as I was sayin', the time has went along. All the while I kept right on reckonin' that Marthy would one day come home again. I felt deep down that her and John Starr wouldn't last out together too awful long. So I waited and waited.

I didn't hear from Johnny and Marthy direct, but Mrs. Morry come by now and then and says they appeared to be gettin' on pretty good, but that Johnny was stove up quite a lot with the rheumatism and was bein' deviled quite a lot by the neighbor people. Now and then the neighbors would willful-like leave his fence gap down so that strollin' cattle could eat up his corn, and hogs would root up his potato bed and garden plot, and all such as that.

But somehow or other, Johnny and Marthy managed for a considerable spell. I heard from 'em now and then indirect-like, sometimes through neighbor people or at the stores. They didn't come here, and I didn't go there. I figgered they'd let me know when they wanted me to come, and they didn't let me know.

So things went on till four years ago last hayin' time. I'd been swingin' a scythe most all day—early August that was

—when Sam Morry's wife come by to tell me that Marthy and John Starr had left the country. Seems as Johnny said he was gettin' tired of bein' took for a cow thief and sheep rustler, says he was goin' back to one of them far-off western states—Montana, or maybe Nevady, I jist now don't surely recollect the name.

Anyway, Mrs. Morry brought me a letter that Marthy had left her to bring. The letter says about the same as Mrs. Morry said, only I was powerful glad to have it said from Marthy. When I read that letter, I knew it wouldn't be long until I had Marthy back with me again.

Well, last Tuesday week, there come a letter from Marthy wrote from far out West in some place—I believe it was Wyomin'. The town had a name like hot pepper. The mail driver left it at Goolsby's store, and it's been left there some little spell before I chanced to go by the store.

I was in such a fidget to get the letter open that I most tore it in two. Marthy said she was comin' home again, that she was startin' to pack up that very next day. Said she'd be some little time gettin' here because she had to sell some livestock to raise the money for to pay bus fare. She said that John Starr had gone off—left her, faded out of her picture. Marthy said she wasn't too much surprised, because for a long time Johnny had been longin' for free roamin' in far-off places. Wasn't that he had dislike against Marthy. He just never was cut out to be a family man. Marthy allows she will keep on loving him—forever.

So that's the how of my sister Marthy. I reckon it's natural for me to do all this gabbin' about her. Because this mornin' when I woke up I had a feelin' like Marthy would be comin' home before nightfall. I bear that same feelin' right now. . . .

BERTIE THE BUM

I have come to believe that the best way to come home to the Ozarks—certainly in the spring or autumn—is afoot. The odds are that October is the most beautiful of the Ozarks months, but May, it seems to me, is the most satisfying for one who knows or would learn the very special loveliness of the back hills, and for this or other good reasons, come back to them.

For May is the special month of Ozarks resurrection. It is a better interval for enjoying the lulling winds and meditating on the hosts of jubilation, as well as joining in the reawakening of the wildflowers in the ever numerous untilled fields and the daffodils and lilacs that bloom again near long-abandoned doorways. In May the rickety porches of country stores find resurrection of their inimitably sincere sociability.

One can just stroll along until the road widens slightly, and there is another affably tired village—possibly Shell Knob, or Ginger Blue, or Hog Eye, or even Monkey Run. Both commercially and socially the general store *is* the town, and its front porch or trading room is the town's forum. For there one meets real Ozarkers who have come together to chew or smoke and to whittle, not purposefully, as with whittling out potato mashers or broom racks, but simply changing sticks of wood into infinitesimal and purposeless slivers while discussing the fishin', huntin' dawgs, politics, the causes of branch-water hard times, and the odd ways of people, not necessarily excepting the reflective commentators themselves.

Now and then one of the store loungers whistles or hums a tune, stretches in the shape of a capital **X** or **Y**, and with easy forthrightness joins in the amiable banter and the mirth that bubbles along like a headwaters spring. The store-porch pause enables one to be on his way, happily refreshed. And as one tramps along, the springtime sunlight begins to lose luster, and the hills begin to change from gold-tinged green as they dim into silken blue. And presently there is an early star to guide by.

My own belief is that the rural Ozarks remain walking country. Such, however, was never the belief or acceptance of Bertie the Bum. Our Bertie excelled at spontaneous and generally purposeless travel; he moved afoot only on very special occasions, such as and including the following, which, at least locally, grew into a pretty tolerable tellin' story.

𝔸PRIL brought the first breath of spring, also Bertie the Bum. It was coming dawn and the town of Aurora, Arkansas, still slept.

The mobile individualist was returned to the frequently sunny pastures of his youth. As a new day came on Aurora, Bertie strolled through the pasture down behind McDonald's poultry house and paused at the banks of Clear Creek where, in his more tender years, it had been his delight to immerse the Lewis children on their way home from Sunday School or the Epworth League cookouts. Then in reverie he strolled up the railway embankment, kindled a cooking fire with an egg crate, and gazed down upon the old home town.

Twenty-nine years had brought their modicum of change to Aurora. A factory stack gave first uprisings of productive smoke. Two ambitious spires, one a real sky-poker of the yellow fire-brick Baptist Church, the other the clock tower of Shakespeare's Fly Rods, Ltd., now peered above the straggling of flat-topped stores. The ugly little bungalows remained as squatty and alien as ever. But now, at last, the streets were stuck down with asphalt, much of it already luridly pitted. On a hillside to the west early sunshine caused the oak leaves to shine with metallic luster.

Yet even as Bertie gazed, the trend of his thoughts changed from nature to nurture; stated more specifically, a fat Dominecker hen strolled around a turn of buckbushes just in time to fall into the determined grasp of prime human need. Bertie rebuilt the fire, and after several minutes of exploring a ravine littered with junk, he located a badly rusted umbrella frame which he patiently converted to a sort of roasting rack. Then he reached into his coat pocket and took out a carefully wrapped packet of ground coffee. Fat roasted hen and strong coffee. Toast was all he lacked.

Far down the lane he saw a hand-lettered sign, which read, "MENGES CASH GROCER—COME IN AND TRY US."

Bertie did. He entered the shop with a beaming "Good morning." Among the shelves of edibles waited a youth with plump pink cheeks and black hair that stood up aggressively like the neck bristles of an annoyed open-range boar.

"A loaf of bread, my fine young man."

It was brought. Bertie sank a thick thumb and forefinger into his right-hand vest pocket and brought forth two thin discs the size of dimes. The one on top was a dime. But the seller got the other one.

Sounds difficult to effect? Actually, it is. But Bertie had spent many a dutiful hour at mastering the technique. Bertie carried one real dime along with a pocketful of steel discs acquired without cost, or the proprietor's knowledge, at a bicycle factory. The trick lay first in showing the real dime, next in hesitating until a welcoming hand is held forth, and finally in drawing attention to higher things just as the substitute is slipped into the seller's palm.

Fat roast hen, coffee, and toasted bread. Bertie picked his teeth with his vest-pocket aluminum toothpick and sank back to rest. South wind played through the new-budded trees, presently roused a faint murmur like the song of a distant ocean. A splotch of white came bouncing up the valley lane and alighted against Bertie's legs. It was most of two pages of a local paper, and reasonably recent. Bertie glanced over its headlines. One of them read:

LESS SMOKE FOR AURORA
Campaign to Last Through Thursday

A cash prize of $1,000, offered by the Cleanliness Committee of the Wake-Up and Get-Up Auxiliary of the Greater Aurora Chamber of Commerce, for the best suggestion on local smoke control, will be awarded at 6 P.M. Thursday, April 2, according to W. Cackletong Whitfield, president of the local Chamber. Suggestions may be entered at the polling place at Owneby's Drug Store until 4 P.M. Thursday. The judges are: Susquehannah L. Root, superintendent of the local gas company; F. Caspar Gollomb, manager of the Aurora Power and Light Company; Newbold S. Furgy, of the Union Electrical Shine-Up Shops.

Bertie pondered. "If they don't want so much smoke, they hadn't ought to build so many fires."

Bertie was beginning to doze when he heard an uncertain step accompanied by a low sob. Looking up, he saw a tearful little boy considerably lost in oversized dungarees and without a shirt. Bertie retired his toothpick and queried gently, "What's wrong, Sonny?"

"I lost Anny."

Bertie felt an odd tremor in the area of his left eyebrow. "Who's Anny?" he inquired.

"Anny's my speckled Dominecker hen."

Bertie set his feet on an exhibit of wing feathers that had grown oddly conspicuous. Quite unusual for him, he momentarily groped for words. Reaching desolately into his pocket, his fingers closed upon the solitary dime.

"Next to Anny, what would you rather have?"

"A white bunny rabbit with pink eyes."

"What does one cost?"

The little man brushed away his tears. "Jimmy Scanzoni says he'll sell his for a quarter."

Bertie's fingers fondled the lone dime. The high resolution arose from within him. He would replace Anny with a pink-eyed rabbit. He would acquire a quarter, even if he had to work for it.

Bertie went forth to earn honorably. At first try he headed for Highland Avenue, Aurora's street of better homes. There his discerning eyes viewed an extensive lawn conspicuously in need of mowing. Bertie strolled up the graveled path and pounded on a ponderous oak door. A sallow, bay-windowed gentleman inquired of his business.

"Mister, for a quarter I'll mow your yard."

The sallow one regarded Bertie much as an irritable elephant eyes a revoltingly puny mouse. "You insolent bum, for less than a quarter I'd hoist your onery behind off my property."

Bertie continued on his way. He next tarried before the shaded premises of Spuggin's Sanitary Rooming House, where a pale, lank female was splitting wood. Bertie doffed his hat and propositioned, "Lady, for a quarter I'd split up the whole pile."

The oppressed one threw away her ax and shrilled, "Hen —ree———a bum!"

At that, a hulking individual in blue overalls got up from

the sunny confines of the front porch and made for Bertie. But Bertie was no longer there.

Down by the railroad tracks, Antwine's Lunch Room was becoming benighted by dirty windows. Once more did Bertie proposition, "Mister, for a quarter I'll wash them winders."

Big Pete Consani, who stood five feet six, ceased pummeling the cash register keys long enough to summon Little Pete Consani, six feet five. Little Pete set down a stand of lard and moved forward, but that, too, was unnecessary.

Rounding the corner of the through street, Bertie read over the gold-lettered poster that hung above the entrance to a drug store: "$1,000 FOR THE WINNER." Again Bertie tarried. A pink-faced gentleman with an expanding vest encouraged his timid advances. "Step up, friend! Contest's open to all. Only a few more hours to vote. Only a couple more to wait. Step right up and hand in your suggestion. Keep it short and, like we always say in Aurora, keep it clean."

Bertie nibbled thoughtfully at the stub of the proffered pencil, then scrawled on the ballot his early morning's reflection: *For Less Smoke, Build Fewer Fires That Smoke.* He considered a while, then scrawled again, so that his final suggestion read: *For Less Smoke, Build Fewer Fires.*

That accomplished, the thinker sauntered back to the more restful premises of McDonald's cow pasture. In time he awoke to gaze out upon settling dusk and a bleary mulitude of street lights. Once more his fingers closed on the solitary dime. No quarter and hardly more than two hours before the passing of the night freight. Then, resolving on a last brave sally, Bertie once more headed toward the contest poll, where he stood and waited.

It was not for long. All of a sudden he became aware that a soft, pink hand was squeezing his own, and almost innumerable hands were whacking his back. Then he was led to the curb where a compact bundle of greenbacks was pressed into his vaguely conscious hands.

"Congratulations, friend of Aurora, on winning the big prize!"

Several things happened during the brief remainder of his short stay in Aurora, town of his boyhood. Among others, Bertie had broken free of the Chamber throng and returned to the moonlit peace of McDonald's cow pasture. As Bertie directed his broad feet in that direction, a rather disgustingly sweet little boy in overlapping dungarees and loosely dangling shirttails had become possessor of enough money to buy two pink-eyed rabbits with a five-dollar bill left over. Also, the *Aurora Daily Beacon*, "Covering Town and Country Like a Blanket of Sunlight," had put out an extra:

CONTEST WON BY NATIVE SON
*Robertus Molier Barger Returns
After 29 Years to Triumph in
Aurora Less-Smoke Award*

Six short words won Robertus M. Barger, former Aurora resident and far-traveled son of this community, $1,000—$166 per word, when his suggestion was awarded the prize granted by the Cleanliness Committee of the Wake-Up and Get-Up Auxiliary of the greater Aurora Chamber of Commerce, as the best suggestion for local smoke control. The judges were unanimous in their decision. In commenting on the suggestion, one judge, Mr. Susquehannah L. Root, superintendent of the local gas company, declared the prize-winning suggestion too profound for immediate comment. Another judge, F. Caspar Gollomb, manager of the Aurora Power and Light Company said:

" 'How shall we build fewer fires that smoke?' The answer is self-evident—use more electricity—the updated replacement for fire." The third judge, Newbold S. Forgy, proprietor of the

Union Electric Shine-Up Shop, said: "Mr. Barger's winning answer carries real thinking. As a substitute for smoking fires, use the harnessed magic of electricity or natural gas! And remember that for every household problem there is a fixture to fit it!"

McDonald's cow pasture was spread over with moonlight. High on the railway embankment Bertie listened to the sweet lullaby of the zimming rails. A subdued tooting sounded from the south—the mating call of a through freight. Bertie sighed in sheer satisfaction.

The sigh was echoed from close at hand. There stood the pink-cheeked, bristly-haired youth from the grocery store, seller of the loaf of bread. For the young there is no gift of greater worth than the gift of good advice. No one appreciated this truth more wholeheartedly than Bertie.

"Well, Sonny, if I shouldn't be seein' you no more, be sure you don't take no wooden nickels"

"Okay, Mister, I won't. And while we're both here, supposin' you take back this phony dime."

WATER POINT

In October of 1926, Arkansas' great poet John Gould Fletcher joined me for several days of comparatively carefree wandering in the back-hill Ozarks. During those days the perceptive lyricist continued to ponder and ask, "What as of now is the most influencing facility in these countrysides?" "Water-powered countryside grain mills," was my offhand, and even then outdated, answer. These had endured in rather astonishing numbers; in 1925 there were no fewer than four hundred. Together we visited several of these folkish converters of home-grown grains to flour, meal, "shorts," "grits," bran, or "middlings." The strong hands, arms, backs, and ingenuity of earlier generations of mill builders had erected enduring monuments, including splendid hardwood water wheels that turned on and on.

Fletcher's own choice was the movable or "peckerwood" lumber mill, at the time almost as numerous as the water-powered grain mills. Following his return to England, the Little Rock–born poet wrote that he had finally decided that in terms of benefits to people the most distinctive of backwoods Ozarks facilities was by then the hydroelectric plant.

Although I presently agreed, the realization came quite belatedly. During my own youth I had never lived with electricity. During my college span and my subsequent dozen years of newspaper work and comparably precarious employment I took the "blessings" of electricity as a matter of course, as well as of routine bill paying. Then throughout the dozen years that followed I worked or loafed in foreign places still largely or entirely lacking in any kind of man-devised illumination; no oil lamps or candles or even open fires. Successively in back-country Honduras, Nicaragua, Guatemala, and lower Mexico, I worked and lived among Indians who had never owned or even used an oil lamp. While serving time in the tribal villages of Equatorial Africa, I was introduced to the traditional strategy of "clapping in" and "clapping out" the night-darkened huts. The first to enter a hut would invariably move in cautiously, all the while clapping his hands loudly. When and if the clapping ceased, his companion or companions would take for granted that the venturer in was being struck down by a death-dealing mamba snake or a leopard or similar real-life nightmare. Accordingly the companion's cue was to dash in to the rescue.

Without prompting from the power industries, whose ethical standards and propaganda handouts I thoroughly detest, my belief holds that the absence of electricity has a great deal to do with keeping "underdeveloped" countries and regions underdeveloped.

For a great many years the same held for the Ozarks. As recently as 1935 barely 2 per cent of Ozarks farm homes had electricity. The prevailing percentage is well above 90. The extensive development of hydroelectric power resources within the areas of chronic need has been an epochal change-maker.

But the harnessing and development of these exceptionally plentiful resources of the region have brought changes for the worse as well as the better. They have profoundly reduced the supply of tellin' stories. They have dealt upset and irreparable loss to a great many individuals, in some instances obliterating entire communities or bringing about the inundation of their economic vitals. Almost invariably the extensive impoundment of water involves the drowning of farm sites, homes, and woodlands. Though it can be a long-range benefactor, the onset of a hydroelectric era is likely to be hard and grim.

"Water Point" is a tellin' story based on fact and, I need hardly confess, remolded as a story for a national magazine.

IF you have never taken a ride with a mountain mail carrier who takes sharply diagonal distances at dully horizontal speeds, you have my word for it that H. Clay Hagood, general manager of the Empire Power and Light Company of Windego, was pleased and relieved to arrive at the back-hill village of Crosses Corner, Arkansas. The same held for Clay Hagood's daughter Phyllis. The two climbed down from the high back seat with audible sighs of relief.

"Thank goodness that ride's over." Clay Hagood paused to light a cigar. "But rough as it turned out to be, the idea of our getting here before the road-building crew was first-rate. Of course, we've got the legal right to start building a road now, but in this sort of deal the personal touch and persuasive tone pay off."

Confidently he turned to his daughter. "Now, if that young man of yours had been the first to get here, he'd probably have blasted out the first mile of roadbed and drilled the base piers for the power dam before he remembered to speak a friendly word to any one of the natives. Sonny Stuart has his good points. But he is still waiting to be filled in on the human phases, like and such as, a construction engineer's got to know people—along with stresses and strains and slide-rule readings and all such."

Father and daughter strolled toward the lone weather-grayed store that was the most evident landmark of Crosses Corner. Phyllis marveled at the remote world into which they had been deposited, the sheer loveliness of the green hills and the gold-misted valley that stretched before them.

"I like it here, ever so much. Any moment I expect to see a satyr or a whole throng of satyrs and maybe some dryads come strolling out of the forest," she confided.

Clay Hagood smiled tolerantly; the whammo those finishing schools do hand out and drum in! "I'm expecting to see something else. To me, all these hills and all this stretch of river spell power produceable at low costs in fair line distances of good markets; also a chance to generate some reserve juice and defenses against heavy drains." Noting that his daughter's interest was less than intense, the power man added more emphatically, "The area has magnificent hydroelectric possibilities. Just wait till we can build a decent road down to here and set in a first-class multi-unit of a generating plant."

"But the country will be different then—all marred with towers and highlines, and the river won't be free anymore. It will be changed, and it won't be for the better."

Clay Hagood preferred to avoid argument with his daughter or, for that matter, with any woman. Moreover, he required information about a lodging place. The storekeeper's answer was not entirely reassuring.

"Not any reg'lar ho-tel hereabouts, mister. Could be you might get lodgings down to Hawkins' Mill. That there's the biggest buildin' hereabouts. Pappy Jim Hawkins went forty year without turnin' ary a traveler away, and young Jim Hawkins that keeps the mill now is right close to the spittin' image of what his pappy was at his age. You just keep strollin' ahead along the river bank, and you can't keep from findin' it."

After almost twenty minutes of walking, the Hagoods came to the shores of an exceptionally long and deep pool. At the lower end of it they found a sturdy dam built of yard-thick white-oak logs. Overlooking the big dam was a rambling and obviously old millhouse, well built of dry masonry sandstone.

Clay Hagood knocked insistently at the heavy oaken doorway. In due course a well-featured and erect young man, dressed in flour-whitened overalls, opened the door. He introduced himself as young Jim Hawkins and listened thoughtfully to the callers' statement of their predicament. "I'd be proud to have you spend the night here. Of course, it's not a hotel, and there'll be no charge. I've done set about cooking a bite of supper."

With that the younger man beckoned the newcomers into a far-spreading front room and began setting a well-scrubbed board table. Phyllis Hagood seemed rather more interested in her host than in supper. But Clay Hagood ate heartily, finished a final buttered biscuit and slice of ham. Then he proffered his host a cigar, and when it was declined, smoked alone.

"How long has your dam been standing?"

Jim Hawkins answered with slow precision, "Mighty close to a hundred years. My folks built it around two years before the Civil War commenced."

Clay Hagood nodded appreciatively. "Always admired virgin white oak as a dam-wall material. Only trouble is we just can't get it nowadays—not for love or money." He added thoughtfully, "I can tell that your dam wall sets on a strategic water point . . . and by the way, I was wondering if this mill might be for sale, at a right price, that is."

"I don't much think it would be."

The power man faced his host. "Well, sir, I've sized you up as the sort of citizen I can and, in fact, like to talk straight business with. So I'm talking straight. My line is electric power—in considerable part from hydroelectric dams. As you may have heard, my company has made a topographical survey of all this valley to show up the best water points. As I just said, your mill is on one such point. Anyway, we know that water power can be generated in this area, put on transmission lines, and sold validly, at least as reserve current."

Jim Hawkins listened, silent as the gathering summer night,

as the power man continued. "Yes sir, we're figuring on building a real effective power dam, a really first-rate steel and cement job maybe seventy feet above channel bed; certainly it would have to raise to sixty."

"I reckon that would do away with the mill and flood just about all the farms between here and the mouth of Plover Creek."

The power man answered thoughtfully, "That could be. As far as your mill goes, we would either have to build the big dam on this site or somewhat directly below it, which would pretty well drown out your location in any case. Anyway, if we were building on your water point here, it wouldn't flood nearly as many farms as it would if built farther downstream.

"But understand this," Hagood continued, "my company stands to pay a fair price, no fooling or fiddling, for every foot and acre of timber or pastureland. It's going to be a fair and profitable proposition for all concerned, certainly not excepting myself. To start with, we are going to build a first-class graded-and-bridged road into this valley—something you never had before. Our power center here will yield a lot of business and a lot of tax money for everybody in the area, a good school for the children, a lot of good jobs. I admire your mill site. I'm ready to offer you a more than fair price for it. What do you think?"

Jim Hawkins answered slowly, "I don't much think it'll work. Folks hereabouts have heard of the idea. They ain't for it."

"But this is the first time the proposition's been mentioned."

"Appears like the folks got wind of it while your engineer fellers were up in these parts last spring."

Clay Hagood studied the ceiling, then Phyllis, then Jim Hawkins. Phyllis was watching the miller. She and her father were come on a mission of peaceful conquest into a strange land that might be turning hostile. She admired the young man's unusual—"quaint" was her choice of an adjective—sincerity. Yet she appreciated the equal sincerity of her father, his intention of doing the fair and businesslike thing. Granted that Phyllis had abiding loyalty to her father and his motives, but at this moment she felt her sympathies edging to the side of Jim Hawkins.

Clay Hagood broke the silence.

"Well, it so happens that we already have a state-approved concession to build the road. Our road-construction gang is on its way here now."

Jim Hawkins strolled across the room, lit another lamp, then hesitated at the dim outline of the loft stairs. "They's rooms up above. Just make like you was to home."

Phyllis tarried to speak good night. "I believe I understand how you feel about the mill and the power dam, and I like your loyalty to your own people."

Jim Hawkins smiled. "Aye, I'm trying for the good of all."

Their hands touched as they parted for the night.

Next morning Phyllis Hagood watched the flowering of a mountain dawn. As she watched she became conscious of the leisurely crunching of slow-grinding wheels, a salutation which told that the miller's day was already well begun.

When the three had finished breakfast, Clay Hagood glanced toward his daughter. "Well, I suppose we'll do some tramping this morning."

Jim Hawkins intervened. "If I was you I don't believe I'd venture out none today."

"Just what do you mean by that?"

"I mean it appears like folks are on the lookout now, and for the next day or two they're liable to be unfriendly-like."

"Well, I've got considerable confidence in you, and since you feel that way about it, I suppose my daughter had best wait here. But for myself, I'm going on about my day's work." He shoved back his chair in a gesture of finality, put on his hat, and sauntered away down the trail.

Within another minute the gathering silence was abruptly broken. A rifle cracked. The newcomer's hat flew high into the air.

Clay Hagood stopped dead still for a moment, then recovered the hat and retreated to the millhouse.

"I tell you, these hillbillies would as soon shoot a man as a squirrel. Look at that hat! If the bullet had hit a couple of inches lower, I guess there'd have been a casualty."

Jim Hawkins took it quite coolly. "I expect maybe that bullet hit just about where it was aimed to hit. It wasn't nothin' but a signal that you hadn't ought to be out strollin'."

Any hour now might see the arrival of the road-building crew and the supply trucks. Sonny Stuart was in charge of the crew—Sonny Stuart, the young construction engineer whom Clay Hagood liked and rather believed he would like as a son-in-law. Stuart would be delivering the goods on time. His reward—probable capture and possible death.

He ought to call out the law. But here there wasn't any law. No way of calling it if there had been. His workmen were coming unprotected and unwarned.

The day wore on in unbearable deliberation.

When Phyllis strolled to a musty window and looked down upon the valley dim in late afternoon sunlight, she turned to her host impulsively. "Tell me, why are you keeping us here? Why are you trying to protect us against your own people?"

"Maybe it's to sort of help about clearin' up a misunderstandin'. People hereabouts don't quite understand. They figure this power dam business is all a city man's smarty trap to take away their land. A country man is apt to think a lot of the ground he lives on. It's all life to him. City folks can't never seem to understand that nor how much us hill folks get obliged to care. That's one side. About the rest—well, come whatever or whoever, I always reckoned visitors is to be looked after and treated fair and neighborly." Jim Hawkins faced Phyllis quickly. "I reckon that ain't quite all of it. I reckon my most reason is you."

Clay Hagood met increasing difficulty in biding the hours. It was past time for the trucks to be arriving. At last he really heard a truck. Within another five minutes he saw a small truck, replete with streaming red flags, its sideboards marked in telling letters, "EXPLOSIVES." Seeing that, Clay Hagood felt a surge of pride. An Empire man had found the way and got through. A slender young man sprang from the seat and hurried up the pathway.

"Good going, Stuart! I'm blamed glad to see you!"

"We're in a tight fix, Mr. Hagood! They had the road blockaded. I had to send the rest of the outfit back to Crosses Corner, or whatever they call it. I brought up the road crew as you ordered—twelve men, four supply trucks, one transport, and the dynamite wagon here."

Clay Hagood motioned the recent arriver into the mill house. Stuart continued his recounting, "Well, we got on okay till we came to that blighted store down yonder. We got the old coot who keeps the store to tell us where you and Phyllis were and started on. But just as we came around that first bend of thick timber, a couple of old plug-uglies with double-barreled shotguns stepped out into the road and told us to halt. Then we saw the whole woods was full of hillbillies with shoulder artillery. They had us beaded, and we had nothing to fight with. I argued, and my foreman argued, but it was just like talking to a clump of oak trees. Finally they told us that if we'd turn around and wait back at the village, they wouldn't bother us. It was about all we could do. But I figured somebody had to get through to you. So, while the other boys were turning, I jumped on the dynamite truck and started her head-on into the blockade. I told 'em if they shot at me we'd all be going to Kingdom Come together. The trick worked. They were afraid of the dynamite. So I zipped through 'em, and came on. Now it looks to me like the thing to do is to get out of here and call for the militia."

Clay Hagood spoke concisely, "That's not my idea of it. We came here to build a dam—not start a war. I don't like to retreat when I know I'm right. My idea is to stay on quietly until we can get things arbitrated."

Phyllis and young Jim Hawkins had appeared somewhat belatedly and together. Seeing Phyllis, Sonny Stuart clasped her hands with a proprietary air that Hawkins was quick to sense. He next greeted the miller with a briefly perfunctory handshake, then turned back to Clay Hagood. "Well, you're the boss. What I'm saying is that it's all a preposterous outrage. Something has to be done right away, and I'd say it'll have to be more than sweet talk."

Jim Hawkins had a suggestion. "If I was you, I believe I'd just wait quiet for a spell."

"I don't get your point."

"I figger you'll save time and bloodshed just by waitin' by. They's victuals here in the mill, enough to last us all quite a few days, if need be. By that time things might be quelled down so you-all can make—what you call arbitrate—with the people. It's a sight better done that way."

"But what the devil do you suppose we'll be doing here all that time—playing mumblety-peg or something? And what about my workmen who are stranded back at what-you-call-it?"

"Long as they wait quiet about Crosses Corner, nothin' will bother 'em. It's the valley grounds that my folks are worried about. Like I told you, you-all are plumb welcome to stay over here. Come times when people save by waitin'. This here's one of them times."

"Got any guns or ammunition?"

"Yes, a musket up over the rafters. But it's not to be used." Having spoken with self-evident finality, Jim Hawkins strolled toward the shedroom door. "I'd best get back to work."

Phyllis joined him. He was busy with corn grinding, guiding ponderous bagfuls of glistening white grain into lines of trough-like hoppers. Presently Jim Hawkins turned from his labor and with a quick thrust of a great wooden lever stilled the turning of the water wheel. Phyllis sensed foreboding. A door had been opened, the outside door, and a hurried inspection showed that the musket was missing from its resting place.

A ring of hoofs outside; then three horsemen galloped down a bend of the trail and slipped out of sight into a cluster of dense underbrush.

Heavy minutes followed. Then a rifle cracked. All the sleepy valley appeared to wake with the ensuing uproar of echoes. The first report was followed by a fierce fusillade of shots hurriedly fired and close at hand. Phyllis joined Jim Hawkins, who waited stolid as an oak. She heard stumbling footsteps outside, and, pressing against the window, she made out a figure staggering toward the mill entrance.

It was Sonny Stuart with a blood-soaked shoulder. He had ventured out in violation of the host's warning and direct order. Obviously, he had shot first—and had come out second best.

There was a very loud splattering of hoofs quite close at hand. A rider came plunging into view; he was waving a long-barreled rifle. He pressed still closer and shouted unnecessarily loudly, "That's jest a samplin' of what's waitin' fer the scum as prowls out to snipe. Could be fer you, too, Jim Hawkins—same as them fancy riffraff you be squirin' with."

With that the rider went thundering away. Jim Hawkins lifted the wounded man. "I'll strive to dress this ripped-up shoulder. It's got to hurt some."

Phyllis and Jim stood at the doorway looking out upon the countryside restored to tranquility.

"What do you think we'd best do now?"

"Jest stay here. We got no choice, now. Should they raid us, make out as best we can. They got us trapped in, and they reckon as how I've turned against 'em, against my own people." Jim Hawkins was sad when he said that.

Clay Hagood joined them; even he spoke a bit uncertainly. "Well, I guess we've managed to hitch you in with quite a batch of trouble. But, like I already told you, we're ready to make good the losses as best we can. And in case of a raid, we're game to stand up and fight to the last ditch."

"If they raid, we'd be damn fools to try fightin'. We're two," he glanced toward the prostrate engineer, "or might be three, against forty or maybe fifty. If they shouldn't get us with musket fire, they could easy burn us out."

"Well, anyway, we've got a truck load of dynamite."

Jim Hawkins seemed oddly unimpressed. "We're trapped in," he repeated. "So is your truck load of dynamite."

It was a painfully long day. Following nightfall and a skimpy supper, Phyllis was much relieved to notice that Stuart seemed free of fever and was sleeping. But she could not sleep.

Toward midnight, when she was at last on the verge of doz-
ing, she roused wide awake again. A light played at the
window, plainly a reflection of fire.

She had gone to bed fully dressed, and rising determinedly,
she headed for a visible shaft of lamplight that crowded
through the doorway of the next room. There she found Jim.
"What is that?" she asked him.

"Signal fires."

"Does it mean they are coming to raid us?"

"I'm fair sure it does. I reckon they'll be comin' against us
from far down the valley way. That's where they're bein'
called together."

Clay Hagood said, "I wonder if now wouldn't be the best
time for us to strike out and take a fighting chance on getting
around or through them?"

The miller shook his head, then with great care lowered
the lamp flame. "That's what they look for us to try. So we
won't. . . . Might be they's one way of getting out, a way
that'll cost the mill." He added matter-of-factly, "But now
it's gone, anyway."

Clay Hagood laid a hand on his shoulder. "Whatever my
company, or let me put it, whatever *I* can do to help——"

Jim Hawkins waited for no further assurance. His tone had
changed to one of steady command. "Might be you could help
me carry in a load of that dynamite. We'll set it down by the
foundation next the dam wall. That way, it'll raze down the
whole dam at one time. I reckon it'll tumble down the millhouse, too. Anyway, when the dam goes, that'll flood all the
valley for a mile down. . . . I've done right considerable work
with dynamite. Reckon I can handle the settin'."

Clay Hagood listened, struck with the sheer audacity of the
scheme.

"Do you plan to set off the charge at the time they raid?"

"Sooner. They'll be comin' up the valley. Down yonder's the line of 'em now—about ready to start. I figger to blow out the milldam before they're plumb on us. That'll flood all the valley underneath. Not drownin' deep, but it'll be sousin' wet, and it'll keep 'em from doing much damage with their firearms." His quiet matter-of-factness gave force to the saying. It was a fight for life now, a struggle against overwhelming odds.

Phyllis spoke tensely, "But don't you see—that would be giving the mill, your home, everything, just for us, strangers who are just taking your hospitality. Why should you give so much—for us?"

"The folks is fightin' mad now. To stay would be coaxin' death. They'd burn the mill and riddle us down with bullets. It's only the choice now of blastin' it down or leavin' them to burn it."

Jim Hawkins, with Clay Hagood as helper, fell to the mission of ruin. Ominous armloads of destruction were carried in stealth, to set by the foundation below the water line. The task finished, Hawkins once more joined Phyllis.

"When time comes to break, I want you here—close by me. And if things get put wrong and we all get brought down, I'd sort of like for you to know——"

He failed to finish, for at a quick impulse he had drawn the girl close into his arms. Their lips touched. For the moment Phyllis forgot all the encroaching dread of danger.

Hagood approached Sonny Stuart, lifted the young engineer to his feet. Hawkins had resumed his post at the window. "Yonder's the way we'll take, up yonder hillside by the right-hand flood gully. High up, there's a clearin'——You-all strike out for it. I'll catch up."

In the valley a cherry-red flash of fire leaped forth. The attacking hill people were moving up the valley way, closing in upon their prey.

Jim Hawkins turned to command, "You all get to the door and be set to run. First I'll give 'em a show to look at. That way they'll be less chance of 'em pickin' us off as we start."

The refugees obeyed. Hawkins vanished and returned with a great armful of dry corn shucks which he placed underneath the window. Then he struck a match to it.

A camouflage of fire. A roar of voices rose from the advancing line of attackers. Then shouts were accentuated by a first fusillade of shots. Jim Hawkins threw open the outer door and commanded his guests to hurry forth. Then he disappeared into the crowding shadows of the millhouse.

Outside, Phyllis led the way, her father following, giving support to Sonny Stuart. Not until they had reached the hilltop clearing did the three look back at the doomed mill. The fire was fast climbing. The line of attackers came on.

A light scurrying of footsteps was close at hand. It was Hawkins. He had set the foundation blast. Now the life of the mill was a matter of burning inches of fuse.

And before anyone could speak, the night was torn apart by a blinding and far-spread pageantry of light, an onrushing, shattering roar. The smoke-clouded sky gave forth a meteor-like shower of falling stone and timbers. A supplementary roar rose as a mighty flood of water broke through the last dim skeleton of the ruined milldam.

When Phyllis had taken her hands from her eyes, she was aware of an infinity of tumbling froth-tongued water spreading over all the valley.

Hoarse shouts and a stray popping of rifles sounded as the first white line of flood water made upon the besiegers, breaking their ranks into disheveled retreat.

Jim Hawkins looked on in silence. His mill was forever gone. The refugees moved on, Phyllis and Jim leading, hands resolutely clasped.

A faintly discernible forest trail led on until at last they were in sight of the village of Crosses Corner.

Clay Hagood paused triumphantly, for now he saw the dim outline of the blockaded trucks. They were placed in a circle, in the center of which the workmen had pitched a rough-and-ready camp. Sonny Stuart waited in self-evident elation. A way was cleared now—a way out. They would come again, come equipped to defend and build and colonize.

But Jim Hawkins had no part in their conversation. He and Phyllis had strolled away from the power builders. They waited together on a nearby mound of rock. On approaching them, Clay Hagood observed that Jim Hawkins' arm firmly encircled his daughter's shoulders.

"Well, now that we've found a way out, I suppose it's time for me to say a thing or two more. You've saved our lives by sacrificing your business, your home. I want to say again that we're ready to make things good to the last dime and penny. And, what's more, if you care to go with us, I can tell you now that the company will have a place for you, a good place."

"I figgered you felt that way about it, and I'm powerful obliged." He turned to Phyllis. "But we've been talkin', and we reckon maybe we'd choose to stay with the hills.

"They's other valleys about. One over west-ways. War Eagle, it's called. Plenty of land there and nobody's settled. Rich, loamy land and a fine lasty river. It'll be ours, I reckon, mine and hers."

TREED

Back in 1927, while laboring as a reporter for the *St. Louis Post-Dispatch*, I covered the manslaughter chronicle upon which this tellin' story is based.

Speaking offhand this would seem to be of the more contemporary vintage of Ozarks tellin' stories. Actually, it is as old as man, thousands and thousands of years older than mortal settlement of the Ozarks. By measures of the living morality of that great and taciturn frontier, most Ozarkers are exceptionally good people; the exceptions are inclined to be violently bad. It follows, and has followed for generations, that Ozarks crimes are predisposed toward the overt and the bloody. For the most part, petty thefts and larcenies are not and never have been excessive in number. Neither have the local practices of confidence games or other slick tricks, nor miscellaneous skulduggery and/or sneakiness. When Ozarkers go wrong, they are disposed to go big and openly, frequently violently or bloodily, wrong. The circuit court dockets continue to sustain this forthright, if sometimes gory, direction.

The precise statement is the more difficult because the impressive preponderance of Ozarks people in towns and rural spaces alike are traditionally both good and law-abiding. But there is a minority of communities, for the most part in the back hills, that may be labeled as "scofflaw." When I was a roving news reporter, I came to know several of these, countrysides where one could anticipate mayhem, or at least a moderately gory stabbing or gang fight within a comparatively brief span of time. These, granted, are exceptional communities; they have never been typical of the Ozarks at large. But they have been a perennial source of tellin' stories, such as the following.

BEING treed by a wild hawg is nobody's play party.

Young Tint Barnes never argued it was, though it had been talked around that he was natural-born muleheaded enough to argy about anything a-tall or nothing whatsomever.

Mostly Mul Sellers did the talking around. Mul, who was—that is, he used to be—Tint's step-pappy, had called the boy downright muleheaded and a lot worse, only Mul Sellers wasn't calling nobody nothing now, on account he wasn't in shape to do so; he was slayed dead.

But joking aside—and who was joking?—being treed by a wild hawg is no fun any time, and this wasn't just any time; it was tree-splitting cold with a norther blowing storm cutting down square across the peach orchard—any damn peach orchard you'd choose to name.

Never before in all his nineteen rough-barked years had Tint Barnes got himself into such a mess-up.

Here it was about the coldest night of the winter and half a dozen before it, and he was treed—like a winter-stiff coon—at the one time in his whole life when he hankered most to get moving. That boy was really treed, and the night, like already noted, was colder than a well-digger's backside at the bottom of the deepest well in all Alasky in January. The Arkansas Ozarks oftentimes get that way in late winter—when, like as not, maybe for days at a time they only got a rusty two-strand barbed wire fence between them and the gizzard-freezing North Pole.

The night kept getting colder. The whole damned world

was sprinkled with snow—froze hard as burnt bacon rinds, and in places it had wind-drifted up to the knee joints of a Injun ten feet tall.

Even in the faint dribbling moonlight Tint could guess that his hands were turning gray blue likewise. It got easier to understand when you recollect that boy was up a blackjack tree and waiting just below him was a winter-starved wild hog. In the hill country or elsewhere a wild hog—gone hungering mean, that is—is the most dreadworthy of all the killers known to man, at any time or season. Even meaner than a mean step-pappy. But Tint was treed for real. As things were shaping up, he was bound to freeze stiff inside the hour. When he stiffened and tumbled down, the wild hog would feast. If he tried to shinny down the tree and run for it, the razorback would be on top him like a lean fast rooster on a slow fat June bug. Painfully Tint lowered a stiffening hand to his belt and touched the barrel tip of his pistol gun. He felt the skin of his fingertips sticking to the cruel metal. The seven-shot revolver still held five bullets.

The other two had lately gone crashing into the balding head of Mul Sellers, his wicked, mean step-pappy.

Tint managed to grasp the pistol stock and to point downward, aiming laboriously. In the rapidly failing light he made out a wavery tier of stiff black bristles. He squeezed the trigger once, then once more. The pistol spat cherry red.

Tint fired again and still again. But the wild hog seemed not to move. Even as he slipped the revolver back into his belt, Tint's gaze stayed with the line of stiff black bristles.

Come to think of it, Mul Sellers only had a little hair; the scant little bit he had left had rose up black and stiff like hog's bristles; truth was, those unparticular bristles had been the last part of Mul Sellers Tint had seen.

Tint Barnes began checking back on where he was or

seemed to be. He sure was up a tree, but maybe it wasn't a wild hawg that had chased him up it. Maybe it truly was Mul Sellers waiting in the bluish snow at the foot of the tree. Maybe the notion that he had been treed by a wild hawg was half-cracked—craziness brought on by freezing.

Maybe from that treetop where he was perishing from bitter cold he was only banging away at a ghost or a killer hant, and that with common lead bullets. If so, he might as well be blowin' kisses. Tint's eyes stayed upon the specter of vengeance.

The mortal Mul Sellers had brought too much of misery to Tint Barnes, likewise to Tint's natural pappy, who had got shot dead in front of his own cabin. But Mul had had an alibi of his whereabouts; brought to court it held tight as the devil's tail is stuck on. And the very night after Mul got sprung out of jail, the old buzzard took to courting Tint's ma. Between June oats mowing time and the laying by of corn that July, Mul took over Barnes's widow, his cabin and clearings, and his little boy, Tint.

From that dark day on, Tint had planned and lived for a time of revolt and rebellion. But against Mul Sellers rebellion didn't come easy. Mul Sellers was the quelling and subduing kind. He had bluing-water eyes set at a mean-looking slant and never exactly focusing. What was left of his head hairs stood up stiff and bristling like a wildcat's bristles. Mul Sellers had an even disposition—he was nearly always mad. But he wasn't crazy enough to go to work. Beginning about the time the Widder Barnes's smokehouse and canning cellar started to get empty, the sheriff hauled Mul in for stealing spoke timbers from the Red Star wagon works and selling them over to Fulbrights' wagon works down at Fayetts-vul. The onery little widget alibied out of it again, only this time he got the whole setup of law men—if you could call them that—suspicious.

Like always, Mul's alibi was real good. The day before he snitched the timbers, Sellers went to Eames' store at Weddington, and, while Storekeeper Eames was out back swapping for some laying hens, Mul lifted off the daily calendar book and stuffed it in his pocket. Then he hit up old man Eames for the loan of a dollar's worth of pin money and put his **X** for an IOU on the calendar page that was showing, meaning the page for the day after. Then the slick tricker spent the rest of the day gumming crackers and cheese and maybe bananas and guzzling barrel cider. On the next day—it being the date of the IOU he'd **X**ed on Eames' calendar—Mul robbered the stocks of spoke timbers, a big wagonload, that is. So he had the calendar writing and old man Eames to witness he'd been loafing at the store the whole day of the stealing.

Inside a month Mul Sellers played the same calendar trick at Eames' store for robbering Lyin' Johnny Wells, the junior hatchet man for a mob of crooked politicians down in Little Rock. When Lyin' Johnny got a bit too flip, Tint's step-pappy creased his head with a cant hook. Lyin' Johnny lived to tell, and this time the calendar trick didn't work out, either. It just happened that the storekeeper had a new granddaughter set for one of those First Baptist foot-tub christenings. It just happened, too, that Preacher Heffelfinger is a fiend about dating papers right. Preacher spotted the wrongness of the calendar leaf, and Mul Sellers got what he had coming, which was ten years at the Tucker Prison Farm—down in the Pine Bluff mosquito bogs. But long before his first year was up, Mul broke clear and headed for the hills and the home he had took over.

He got there mean-set with a jug of corn licker under his belt. He hadn't much more than got inside the lean-to when he charged Widder Barnes with carrying on with Parson Heffelfinger whilst her lawful husband man was down at the penitentiary paying off his debt to society and whatnot. When the widder said she hadn't neither, Mul started to work her over with a broom, including the handle end of it. That was where young Tint Barnes came back into the picture. He eased up to the loft, slipped the revolver from underneath his shuck mattress, and emptied two cartridges into Mul Sellers' silly-looking head.

After that Tint remembered slipping the pistol gun into his belt and striking out in the bitter cold night and heading in the general direction of higher above and farther away. He recollected, too, that while he was patting down the log road that skirts Seamsters' seeps, the wild hog charged out from a grove of haw bushes and made for him like a believing Israelite after an unbelieving Hittite.

That was when he ought to have shot it out, only Tint was a scared-up boy, and in place of more gunnery he up and ran for it. That stubby blackjack tree was all the far he could get. He upleaped for the stubby trunk and kneed in to climb it. At the first scruff he saw the mean hog raising up behind him, tusks shining in the sickly moonlight, mouth open most as wide as a cookstove door. Fronting the knife-sharp twigs that clawed into his face and belly, Tint scrunched on to the first sizable limb, but he could get no higher.

Now, after like two hours of the crucifying cold, there he still was—with an empty pistol gun and underneath him was a mean wild hog—from the looks of it maybe a killer ghost, or hant, or ever which way you would choice to name it.

As he looked down again at the hunched specter with the upstanding bristles, Tint Barnes became aware of a stinging fire that seemed to rise from his eyes and nostrils and, by painful stages, to spread down his throat and into his chest. If he were freezing to death—and what else could this be?— it was a far ways off from what people had said. For here he was being practically roasted alive by what looked a lot like a real and true fire.

Tint tried to raise a free hand to his face. It might be, of course, that he was already froze to death. It could be he perched in another kind of hell. Another kind of . . . . Dazedly Tint found himself remembering the spirited advice of Parson Heffelfinger, who had pointed out, "You ain't never been saved, Tinty Barnes. You ain't never been bathed in the Blood of the Lamb."

Tint figured at the time, and still did, that bathing in sheep's blood is a mighty silly thing to be doing. Come to think of it, what's too wrong about water and maybe a daub of soap if a person is hell-bent on bath taking? Tint recollected reminding the preacher that he hadn't never stole nothing nor killed nobody, which back at that time was the Gospel truth, but anyway, why get nastied up with sheep's blood? It for sure wouldn't be doing any favor to any lamb either.

Preacher Heffelfinger passed that one by, but kept drumming at him. "You ain't yet been saved, Tinty Barnes. And onless you mend your way you're headed smack dab straight fer hell!"

"You mean, I'd wake up down yonder with my step-pa, Mul Sellers, hard by?"

Preacher Heffelfinger's answer was dimmed by caution, understanding, and an exceptionally big mouthful of tobacco juice.

"Mebbe they's another kind of hell I could go to jest on my own?" Tint had asked almost pleadingly.

Though the parson had appeared to nod as he spat, Tint was never entirely certain of it, but anyhow, maybe this here was the other kind of hell. . . . Even so, and hell and hog hants notwithstanding, the youngster yielded to the urge for a last try with gunplay.

Treed

He had started out with a seven-bullet pistol gun full-loaded. He had let his step-pappy, Mul Sellers, have two. He'd let the hog shape have four. That left one bullet, least ways it ought to.

Tint stamped the tree limb with the freezing clods that appeared to be his feet and again lowered his right hand into his belt, took up the revolver, again aimed shakily into the dim moonlight, then managed to close a stiffening forefinger on the trigger. A great red blaze tore into the night. The specter hog only waited—still as a dead oak stump.

The empty pistol slipped from Tint's hand. A great aching returned to his head and chest. His legs seemed to be falling out from under him.

As well as Tint Barnes could figure it out, he was waking up in hell. Preacher Heffelfinger had been righter than rain. Furthermore, and at long last, the cold hell seemed to be changing over to the hot kind. There was a fiercely hot fire squarely in front of him, but it smelled not of brimstone but of cedar wood.

Tint couldn't catch as much as one solitary scent of sulfur. But the fire really was hot. He struggled back from it, and then he heard a thing that somehow did not seem to belong in hell. It was his mother's voice. That wasn't a rightful development. There wasn't a mite of sense or justice in bringing the Widder Barnes to perdition. She never killed nobody nor stole nothing. Also, she had been saved at more protracted camp meetings than the cat has whiskers.

Next, Tint made out another voice, a sort of sing-song that he presently recognized as belonging to Sheriff Henry Walker from up at Jasper town. He wasn't by any means astonished at finding the Sheriff man in hell; but to find the Sheriff making easy talk with his mother, and neither one seeming to be feeling any pain . . . that was real peculiar.

Tint was hardly less surprised to find hell such a pint-size sort of a place, hardly bigger than the hearth of a fireplace. By gradual stages he began to notice that hell-fire looks a lot like the common, ordinary fireplace kind, including the rock side-walls and red cedar mantelboard a lot like those in the Barnes cabin.

But when he recognized the maplewood clock that he had been raised by, Tint peered less fearfully around the room. First he looked at the Widder Barnes, then at the Sheriff man. And though it hurt to try, he next found that he could still speak. "Was that there a hawg I was tryin' to shoot before I come here?"

Sheriff Walker appeared to be grinning. "Sonny, it *was* a hawg. . . . And you shore as hell shot it. I found you piled down in the snow square in front of the crittur. I walked up and gave the hawg a kick, and it toppled over like a daid rotted stump. I taken out my flashlight and counted five bullets put square between the hawg's eyes in a space about the size of a dollar piece.

"So I fetched you in. Another ten minutes you'd been stiff dead as that wild razorback was. I drug in the hawg, too. Left it on the porchway beside your dear dee-parted step-pa."

The sheriff's puckered grin lingered. "You might say you done a right apt shootin' job on both of them killers."

With immense effort Tint sat upright and scooted himself away from the towering fire. "But Mul Sellers wasn't no killer."

Sheriff Walker continued to finger Tint's revolver. "You might say he was so, sonny. Seems your dear dee-parted step-pa slew a penitentiary guard whilst takin' off from the Tucker Farm down Pine Bluff way."

With visible unsteadiness Tint got to his feet. "Meanin' I don't get hung?"

Sheriff Walker's grin broadened. "You might say it *could* mean that, sonny." With great care the Sheriff man again looked over the pistol gun and handed it back to Tint. "You can keep that there thing for to stalk bunny rabbits with. Sure ain't no need to stalk Mul Sellers no more. State wanted Mul took in. You shore as hell took him in—same as that wild hawg. I'm taking along the hams and shoulders and tenderloin and bacon sides and leavin' you most of the rest—you might say as a ree-ward."

Widder Barnes almost smiled. "That there is mighty kindly from you, Sheriff. Hit leaves fer Tinty and me the spareribs and the makin's of headcheese and we relish 'em both." The thin shoulders swayed with unusual determination. "Sheriff, you was speakin' of a ree-ward. While ago when Mul was a-whalin' me with that there broomstick, he was yellin' that the state was offerin' three hunderd dollars ree-ward for takin' him dead or alive. Said he was cloutin' me so as I couldn't get to the preacher man to tattletale. He said Parson Heffelfinger would for sure be a-gettin' three years of preacher's pay from pidginin' on him and takin' the ree-ward. . . . Reckon that there was silly talk?"

"You might say it was, Miz Sellers—I mean to say Miz Barnes." The Sheriff's smile seemed permanent.

Tint's ma gulped hard. "So, Sheriff, so what comes of that three-hunderd-dollar money ree-ward?"

For a moment the Sheriff's smile wavered. "You might say it will somehow be gettin' lost in channels."

The Widder Barnes looked at the law man more closely. "Sheriff, I jest don't foller that fancy lawyerin' talk hardly a-tall. But by any happenchance, would you be a-sayin' that ree-ward money maybe will get dropped by somebody into some river and let get floated away in the wrong channel?"

"You *might* say that, Miz Barnes. You might say that there is already happenin'. Jest as sure as you be settin' there and I be standin' here you might of said what you just now said."

TIMBER MAN

Through the years, excepting only the people and the rivers, timber has remained the greatest natural resource of the Ozarks. Timber is a story-making resource. It makes for hard and sometimes chancy work, demanding of skill, experience, and a lonely man's determination. At times it also requires group work and an unusual quality of leadership.

The special-use timbers such as white oak, the great king of the hardwoods, have required special kinds of men. John Spencer, the principal character of the ensuing story, was such a man, one who spoke and acted for the working advocates of elementary conservation. Practically speaking, timber is the most durable of major plant life. Trees have flourished and sheltered on principal areas of the earth for hundreds of millions of years before man arrived. John Spencer was one who conceded that timber may continue to grace and protect our plundered planet innumerable centuries after man has departed from it. But, as one who believed that the only El Dorado the Ozarks ever had was its woods, John Spencer was discreetly but zealously determined to proselytize in deed for his particular devotion.

The tellin' story which follows is mostly factual. Except for some name changing and arbitrary renaming of whereabouts, in keeping with the queasy mandates of magazine fiction (this story was a fiction entry in a once corpulent but long since deceased "popular" magazine), the not especially scintillating narrative might have been printed in the local newspaper, had there been one.

JOHN Spencer was a timber man—changed from a back-woods axman to general manager of one of the nation's mightiest lumber firms. He was coming back to his boyhood home as a timber man.

Eight country miles waited between Baldwinville, a county-seat town with a railroad station, and Red Star, Spencer's birthplace and his long-time home. Tired sunlight poured through the treetops now thinning with late autumn. For his own good reasons the homecomer chose to travel those miles afoot.

It had been a third of a century since he last walked the old Red Star road. What he remembered as young fruit orchards had grown old. Roadside saplings were changed to mature trees. And thirty-two years spent mostly in offices were making the eight miles seem long. The first six miles had taken an hour and forty minutes. Not bad, but not really good. He presently noticed that only one store remained at the Red Star crossroads, a time-battered, lurch-roofed wooden building with a big and somewhat dingy front window marked "POST OFFICE   GEN MDSE   EAT."

The homecomer followed the latter suggestion. Having tried a ham sandwich that was made with slightly stale bread, he fed the scraps to an amiably sniffing hound and paid the tab. The white-haired storekeeper rested heavily on the counter. "'Pears like I've seed you before. Say the name is Spencer?" The homecomer had not said. But the storekeeper yawned his recognition, "Shore, you're Tom Spencer's boy!"

"The older one."

"Yes, they was a younger one. We lost him in the Big War. Name was Don." The storekeeper lighted his fire-blackened pipe. "Yessir. Don's widow and boy and girl live down on the old place in the Holler."

"That's where I'm headed."

The storekeeper puffed hard. "Then you'll be gettin' thar just about in time for the log-burnin'."

"The what?"

The storekeeper explained casually. "Neighbor folks be clearin' a patch of land to help with the new school the deestrict aims to keep. They already built a right nice shack schoolhouse. Miz Annie Spencer, your sister-in-law, she figgers to teach the school. She allowed she'd teach for reasonable little, but they wasn't that much left after the buildin'. So Annie turned over a woodland forty that neighbor people has agreed to farm on shares and give the earnin's to he'p with the school. They figger on plantin' the ground to strawberries and maybe, later on, some orchard fruit."

"Which forty are they clearing?"

The storekeeper spat thoughtfully. "Seems I recollect it was the forty to the northeast."

John Spencer frowned. "But there's fine timber in that plot!"

The storekeeper puffed on easily. "Yessir, don't doubt there's walnut and some oak and likely some hickory, but no real loggin' goes on hereabouts no more. And that forty is good ground and it would make good crops. Uncle Sikes Williams that runs a stave mill up to Huntsville agreed to bring his crew down and help fell the timber. It's mostly all down by now. But it lays too far out from Fayetts-vul town to sell for firewood, so the people estimated the best way was just to burn hit off and set about breakin' the ground for crops now while fall weather holds. They're most ready for to set the big log-burn."

The storekeeper was surprised at the abruptness of his customer's departure. Must be the way a city turns a man—abrupt-like and untalking.

Going home. A redbird perched on a swaying dogwood branch. Newly fallen leaves swished across the dimming road. John Spencer enjoyed the walking; it enabled him to walk in stride with his lost boyhood. Presently he stopped beside a broad stump, long dead and weather blackened. He and his younger brother, who was twelve at the time, had felled that tree in the course of the last week that John Spencer had spent at home. The homecomer also remembered that the following Saturday night Squire Taggert had a housewarming "favoring" his daughter Annie and her thirteenth birthday.

Both the Spencer boys had been among those present. While the Squire was showing them in, John noticed that Annie smiled in his direction. He next noticed that his younger brother Don was standing just behind him. A timber man guides by small observations. Seven years later his brother Don up and married Annie Taggert. The following year the couple took over the old Spencer homestead and settled to farming.

John had intended to go to the wedding, but just at the time the mill had sent him to measure off some side-mountain sections of spruce in Washington State. So, in lieu of his presence, John had mailed his congratulations, best wishes, and most of his then available savings—about seven hundred dollars—to help the young couple refurnish the old house and buy needed farm equipment.

He had mailed his congratulations, well wishes, and somewhat larger checks on being advised of the successive births of the couple's daughter, Young Annie, and, less than two years thereafter, their son, Young Don. During the Big War, which he remembered as World Brawl One, John Spencer acquired a commission as a procurement officer for the Army Quartermaster Corps directly after his brother Don enlisted in the army. Don fought his last battle at Belleau Wood.

John shuffled on past Armistice Day as a major in what he termed the Waste Basket Brigade.

A light wind swayed the browning oak tops, and a murmur rose, like the song of a distant ocean. As he rounded the next bend, the homecomer noticed that the road was no longer empty. Before him walked a farm boy dressed in blue dungarees loosely fitted and rather abundantly patched. As he increased his pace, the homecomer noticed that the youth had sandy red hair that persistently defied the repressive brim of a very hard-used felt hat. The farm boy turned, smiling. John Spencer could have sworn by cords and carloads of Bibles that the smile belonged to his younger brother.

Rather cautiously he joined the youth. "So you are young Don Spencer."

The farm boy answered easily, "Yessir, that's right. How'd you know it?"

The timber man felt a great urge to pull the youth into his arms but repressed it. "I'm your old uncle."

The boy smiled. "Proud to know you."

They followed the leaf-littered road on down into Red Star Hollow. Coming home . . . . They tramped into the green yardway. The old house waited, weather beaten and serene. Young Don hurried to the door and called out the news. John Spencer strolled inside. The fireplace showed a dim remnant of embers, but the use-battered wood box was well laden in readiness for the chilly night that would soon be on them.

"Just set down! Expect Ma and Ann is back in the kitchen somewhere."

A swishing of skirts and clacking of heels verified the expectation. Don's Ann and Young Ann! John Spencer got to his feet. The years had brought rather remarkably little change to the mother. Her hair was graying, but her eyes and her body molding remained youthful. When he saw Young

Ann, John recalled vividly the sight of her mother at Squire Taggert's housewarming.

When greetings had been duly exchanged, Don's Ann suggested that the menfolks build up the fire in the fireplace and set about comfortably while she and Young Ann finished getting together a snack of supper. John Spencer suggested that he and Young Don join in the good and necessary getting together of a snack. They did. The kerosene lamps were lighted, and the cookstove purred with a freshly kindled fire. John began setting the table while Young Ann discreetly counseled. He liked the work. He liked it all the more when a gentle spluttering in the big frying pan told that corn mush was being fried—changed by fire magic from chill white to a deliciously aromaed golden brown—in company with thick slices of pork tenderloin. John breathed in the aromas, took down a long-used earthenware coffeepot, and began filling the holder with home-ground coffee.

By the time the coffee was made, the rest of the meal was set. The four filed into the dining room where each took a side of the small square table. Ann spoke grace. John found the food satisfying, the company delightful. Supper finished, Ann cleared the table while Don piled dead wood into the sitting-room fireplace. When the dishes were washed, the four drew up chairs and talked until the fire had passed from frolicsome youth to puttering old age.

In the course of the talk John Spencer got around to the new school and the timber clearing.

For the most part the storekeeper had been substantially correct. The schoolhouse was almost completed, but as yet there was nowhere near enough money to keep school with. Ann had agreed to teach at least for the first year. Before marrying she had completed the two-year course at the teachers' college in Fayetteville; she had earned what was then known as a C.L.I.—Certificate for a Licensed Instructor. She had very personally deeded the wood lot forty acres to the school district. Most of the tree felling had been done. The whole countryside, including Uncle Sikes Williams' stave crew, would be back next morning to complete the cutting and begin the burning. The neighbor people were agreed that burning was the best and easiest way to clear the land, particularly now that there was no longer much of a market for log wood and even less for fuel wood. John Spencer wanted to say a great deal. But he noticed that Ann was beginning to glance toward the mantelpiece clock, and he wished to find some time to himself for careful thinking.

Next morning he was awake very soon after daybreak; even so, breakfast was waiting, and Ann was already beginning preparations for a workmen's picnic. Young Ann was stuffing shoe boxes with thick meat sandwiches in preparation for Uncle Sikes and his woodsmen, who would shortly be arriving to help with clearing the school land. Breakfast was barely finished when early-rising neighbors began arriving.

"Maybe you'd like to come out and meet our home folks," Ann suggested.

"I'd like that. But first off, I'm having myself a fast stroll through that timber patch."

Ann smiled her consent. John hurried out into the new autumn morning, noting that early sunlight gave a wonderful green-gold sheen to the open pastures. He walked on until he came to a great rectangle of ready-felled trees. As he walked through the fallen timber, he began to estimate that not far from a fourth part of the available saw logs was walnut; for good measure there was some excellent oak, hickory, ash, and yellow birch in saw-log size.

The volunteer choppers had cut some small part of the locust, mulberry, and bois d'arc into six-foot lengths for fencing posts. But the great bulk of the harvest was ready doomed to burn. John Spencer shuddered at the fantasy of waste. Then he reflected that these were farming people. In this area commercial logging had pretty well played itself out a long generation earlier; it was failing even when John Spencer left. Red Star was changed to a farming community, and, in their timeless way, farmers compute and foresee work in terms of planted fields and pastures.

A timber man's job is to harvest and market the valuable trees. John recognized that here and now his job, in fact his duty, was to recover and put to use the usable timber now on the ground. As he glimpsed it, his own term was eyeballed it, no less than eighty thousand board feet of marketable logs were already felled. If properly recovered and marketed, there was enough high-value timber to pay the teacher and otherwise keep the countryside school for at least a couple of years, maybe longer. For with special-use timbers, a quick guess is usually an underestimate.

But the recovery would not be easy, especially now that time was running out. He had some tall persuading to do. He was now an outsider; speaking Ozarkwise, a third of a century of continuous absence makes anybody an outsider. And this school was their idea, their business.

Back in the yardway John joined what seemed to be an open reunion of the entire Red Star countryside, including its backwoods fringes. The homecomer recognized many of the old-timers, beginning with Squire Taggert, now white haired and stooped, and Tola Sumerlin, who used to carry the mail by saddlebag, now gray and almost blind and long ago "pensioned off" by the U.S. Post Office Department. He greeted several rural grandmothers whom he had last seen when they were builders of mossbank playhouses and deputized borrowers of vinegar and salt and clabber milk. All in all, the company was welcoming, including even the pre-teen-agers who brought along their dogs that smelled of distant spaces and vanquished skunks.

Presently Uncle Sikes Williams and his five-man stave crew came tramping down the road, all big men, evidencing the good-natured conceit of countryside strong men. Uncle Sikes, a white-haired, leather-brown giant of a man, took the homecomer's hand in a bone-crunching grip. Then, in a jovial bellow, Uncle Sikes allowed that, since everybody was there and work brittle, the right thing was to go forth and "sot" the timber. Tola Sumerlin tottered forward and interrupted. "'Scuse me, Squire! Figgered mebbe Johnny Spencer might have a notion or two to tell us. He knows right considerable about timber—he's 'bout the highest up they is in that line."

John took advantage of the lull to speak very cautiously, "I was walking your clearing just now, did some quick eyeballing of the felled logs. I see there's considerable walnut growth and other marketable saw logs. If we could sort the timber, get the logs to a railhead——"

Squire Taggert interrupted. "We don't no longer have no log markets hereabouts, Johnny. Ain't been so much as one timber buyer through here in, I 'spect, twenty year. . . . We purty well picked out the post timbers yesterday. And there ain't no longer a sale for cordwood—nohow not when it's got to be long hauled." The old man cleared his throat. "So my notion is we better get ahead with the burnin' off so as we can get the ground plowed 'fore heavy freezes commence."

There was a murmur of agreement. Uncle Sikes Williams boomed his own. "I go along with the Squire about not wastin' no more time gettin' the ground cleared. Fact is, I'd cherish to see some strawberry plants sot out 'fore freezes commences." The big man paused and spat. "Course, this young feller standin' next to me could be right. . . . But I got to say this, them logs he speaks about wouldn't do *me* no good. I only keep a peckerwood sawmill for cuttin' barrel staves and wagon and plowshares timbers out of oak. Reg'lar lumberin' I jest don't know and don't do." Uncle Sikes paused diplomatically. "Now me and my boys only come down to help along as best we can for Miz Annie and the school. We don't pree-tend to tell nobody what they'd ought to do——" The big man paused again. "But one thing I will say—we all need to have a boss on this job; one man, that is, who gives out the orders. That there goes for any job."

"How we best elect a boss?" Squire Taggert asked.

"Well, Squire, now us peckerwoods," Uncle Sikes designated himself and his crew with one wag of his right thumb, "when they's no boss ready app'inted on a tree-fellin' job, we generally always have a choppin' contest, and the one that can halve a good log first with an ax, he takes over as boss . . . on account whatever else he don't know about, he's got to know somethin' or other about short-log handlin'.'"

The proposal seemed reasonable. John Spencer remembered it as long orthodox practice in logging camps of an earlier but long since departed generation. But he also remembered that he himself had not actually chopped or "axed through" a log in years—more years than he cared to admit. He had been a first-rate axman, say, twenty years ago. He knew that, and skill with an ax is a lasting skill; but the requisite muscles and breath are something else again.

Uncle Sikes Williams was speaking again. "Tell you what let's do, folks! Suppose I pick one of my boys and match him up with the young gent here alongside me. Then we'll pick us two equal-size logs, and if my boy wins the choppin', we'll have Squire Taggert take charge, and if this visitin' gent wins, then he'll be boss of the whole works."

Again the crowd's approval was evident. Uncle Sikes concluded. "So I pick that young feller over yonder with them baby-doll blue eyes. Goes by the name of Bill Plue."

The homecomer eyed his opponent-elect, a raw-boned and kindly-featured young giant who was leaning heavily on a long-handled ax. John noted that the ax was double-edged, as the local designation had it, "double-headed," and that both cutting edges were whetted until they sparkled in the early morning sun. He knew a good ax when he saw one; also an able competitor. And he knew that his own situation called for gumption and a good ax.

He saw Young Don bringing the last named. John Spencer took the ax, viewed it approvingly, though it was small and single-edged. It was beautifully sharpened and set to a home-made hickory handle that was thin, new, and gracefully curved. The homecomer felt the cutting edge—he called it the "bite"—with an appraising thumb. The edge was deftly tapered, yet it had a slight but savage roughness. It was unquestionably a good ax superbly sharpened. John shouldered the tool and fell in step with his appointed rival.

Uncle Sikes led the way to the clearing and located two big logs, each a good thirty inches thick and lying within ten paces of the other. Each happened to be red oak, the only two "lays" of that remorseless hardwood then in view. On each log he notched the bark a handle length in from the butt and let the contestants draw straws for logs.

The onlookers, whose numbers kept growing, began to form a half-circle. John Spencer knew that he was being sized up as the dark horse of the contest. Very frankly that was his own estimate. But as he took his place and made certain of footing, he resolved to fight for it. He was a timber man and these were his people. . . . And Young Don, in particular, was behind him, ax and heart.

"Ever when I drop this old hat, you two commence choppin'!"

Uncle Sikes Williams lifted off his battered felt hat and slammed it to earth. John Spencer lifted his ax in an easy arch and brought it down with all his might. The blade sank a good two inches into firm sapwood. He had struck the first lick. He pulled the ax clear and, flattening the sweep of his strikes, cut straight down, shaping a niche side.

Bill Plue was in action now, swinging leisurely but hard. His axhead flashed in morning sunlight, and descended and rose again in almost perfect cadence. Bill Plue was trading edges, slipping the handle in midair, so that each successive blow landed with an alternate cutting edge. That's an advantage of a double-edged ax. Shifting the cutting edge delays the inevitable dulling.

But John Spencer had always favored plain axes—he believed they balance better. He increased his swing for the right-hand side of the cut. One, two, three—faster, and not so hard. He paused to shed his jacket. Silly not to have thought of that sooner. One, two, three—slope and straight. Heartwood was showing now. Red heartwood, and the log was half in two.

John Spencer changed sides. So far he was ahead. In turning he glanced upward to a blurred pageantry of faces. One he saw clearly—Young Don's, features tense and tremendously hopeful. There was no doubt that the boy was for John Spencer, and no doubt that John's rival was a real axman. Even so, his deft handle-turning was taking time—perhaps only hundredth parts of seconds, but even that little was telling.

But so were John Spencer's years of sitting in offices. Pains shot through his shoulders and chest, and his wrists were beginning to ache from the recoil. A good axman never forgets how to use an ax. The rub lies in keeping up the power and the timing. He was now quite certain that he had the better ax. The cutting edge was superb, the home-made handle delicate and thin, shaped right to allow the hands to slide easily, recoil easily. One, two, three, four, five, six, seven. Chips flew like oversized bullets.

But no ax can win a chopping contest by itself. Red blotches were playing before John's eyes. Sharp pains were ripping through his shoulders. Yet he had to win . . . had to win. If he could only get the bossing of this labor force, he'd get out enough salable logs to keep the school going maybe a passel of years. And he would prove to his people that he was one of them and, for good measure or bad, a real timber man.

John sobbed for breath. He had to win. By all that was good and holy he was *going* to win. Now he had cleared all the heartwood. Daylight showed through the log's middle. Three more licks would finish it. There they were. One and two. And three. And there was the log square in two.

Bill Plue was still chopping. As he sank to the cushiony earth, John heard two final strokes of his rival's ax. He had won by barely two licks. If Bill Plue had not taken time for his fancy handle twirling, John Spencer would have lost—easy, meaning, of course, hard. Had there been another log to chop—but there wasn't. John Spencer was the winner. He was aware of a racing pulse, of an unfamiliar roaring in his head. Bill Plue had finished as cool and steady as if he had been whittling a match.

John Spencer glanced toward his nephew, who looked on in elation. Uncle Sikes Williams made expert perusal of the winner's cut. "Done a right good job! That straight edge looks like it was ripped out with a power saw."

Bill Plue strolled forward grinning. "Reckon next time I'd ought to chew out punkwood."

"You did all right. Came close to winnin'."

Young Don joined them. "It sure was mighty good choppin'."

"With an ax like yours it was really nothin'."

But it was something; John Spencer knew it was. He knew, too, that it was time to act. As soon as he had regained his breath, he stepped to the big stump and faced the crowd.

"All of you are helping. And here is how it's going to be: You came here expecting to work one full day. Instead, you're going to work two full days, and I'm going to work at least four. We're not burning anything except the brush. We are going to take out all the salable logs, even the salable pulpwood, which we'll saw into four-foot logs. Since we are going to market all the timber logs, we might as well really clean up the works.

"First thing we're going to do is build a loading dock on the west slope of yonder little hill. While Uncle Sikes and his men are starting the dock, I'm going to drive to the county seat. I'm going to rent a heavy diesel tractor and buy drag cables for snaking out the heavy logs. Besides that, I'm going to buy a dozen cant hooks for you strong boys to roll and load with. Also, I'm going to hire heavy trucks to begin hauling logs, starting this afternoon. By that time the railroad freight agent is going to have a string of flatcars on siding ready to take on logs.

"I'm also renting a couple of chain saws in Fayetteville; they'll speed up the work, help us get in more timber in less time. We won't be wasting a stick. We'll burn nothing but the rubble."

Sensing approval, John Spencer continued, "I'm personally paying for all the rentals and extra equipment required on this job. This is my own offering to the new school. I'm going to sell all the timber, including small stuff, for top dollar on the best markets now available. I'm not buying or taking commission. All the money will come directly here; Squire Taggert will be treasurer. I'll be missing my guess if the take, including the walnut, is less than fifteen thousand dollars. Every dime and penny of it goes to the school. . . .

"Any questions? No? I'm dividing all of you into six work squads; I'm making Bill Plue leader of the long-log squad. Uncle Sikes will be the loading boss. So, let's roll! Pick your squads and move out!"

It was late morning when John Spencer returned from the county seat. He was using Ann's aging sedan to lead a caravan of heavy trucks, all stripped and pillared for log hauling. One truck carried a shiny green tractor equipped with a drag cable and hoist. Another carried a twenty-foot rubber-wheeled wagon. The sedan was piled with an unusual assortment of groceries, hand axes, cant hooks, chain saws, cans of gasoline, and tins of lubricants.

Gingerly the homecomer climbed to the tractor seat, started the diesel engine, and steered the green monster with caterpillar treads out of the truck bed to a roadside bank. As he headed the tractor through the pasture gate and beckoned the trucks to follow, he saw that a log-built loading dock was already taking form; also that long logs were already being rolled to a newly shaped skidway back of the loading dock.

John Spencer called to Young Don and directed him to distribute the cant hooks, new axes, and chain saws, after first putting the groceries away. He directed the trucks to form a line in front of the dock. Then he slipped from the tractor seat and attached the drag cable to the end of a big walnut log. He remounted, began snaking the big log to the skidway. Then he headed the tractor to a deep ravine where at least a hundred big logs waited recruiting.

As he picked his way among the felled trees, he saw cords of limbwood rising, and he listened to the crack of many axes. Good work well begun. Two round trips to railhead by four trucks during the afternoon would put better than sixty thousand feet of saw logs aboard train by nightfall. Three hauls tomorrow would pretty well finish the long logs; then another dozen loads of pulpwood would clear up the job. He would hire another tractor tomorrow. Also another pickup wagon.

He listened to the chain saw roar into action, then he slipped the cable loop on another big log. He liked the work . . . liked the people. A long afternoon was coming up—and a whopper of a day tomorrow.

As soon as all the timber was loaded out, he would have the land tractor-plowed. But the big job of timbering would be done, and well done, mostly by good neighbors. As he headed the big tractor and the bigger log behind it to the skidway, John Spencer waved to Young Don, who was chopping manfully at an immense oak top. Soon enough John Spencer, being a timber man, would have to be going back to his own job. But he would go with the certain knowledge that he was still one of the Red Star folks.

COMPROMISE

Ozarks tellin' stories have propensities for beginning in April. As a far-roaming newspaper correspondent I learned long ago that in the Ozarks at large April is also the year's apex for violent crime, violent storms, fist fights, wife beatings, and comparatively crowded jails. One of my kinsmen who used to be employed by the U.S. Bureau of the Census affirmed that in the Ozarks more births occur during April than any other month. My cousin Allan contended that this was so because April follows the fervent climax of the late summer revival or protracted church meeting by nine months, or 270 days—the customary interval of human pregnancy. However pertinent or impertinent the explanation, I don't really believe it, though certainly I cannot deny having been due to have been born in April myself— as usual, I was late.

Even so, I have long since accepted that Ozarks Aprils, however beautiful or terrible or benevolent or violent, are calendar registries of memorable beginnings, of the farming season with newly foaled livestock, first garden greens, and timidly pink strawberries. And it is the time of country-school vacations. Land transfers also reach a high mark in April, and so, alas, do foreclosures. And for many years, at least in the backwoods Ozarks, April has been the number-one month for immigration. This obviously well-motivated entry has an understandable role in Ozarks tellin' stories. "Compromise" is a rather cogitative recounting of the occasional recurring phenomenon of a lone comer with a revived love of land and a sizable burden of noble intentions. Here, again, the recounting is essentially factual, despite the changing of names and place names.

HANS Gernstacher had left his native Austria so long ago that he could remember in very early childhood when the great Blue Danube was at least recognizably blue. That was no longer the case in 1920 when Hans, then nineteen, set forth, as he later put it, to discover the world. His routes of discovery were never easy and rarely comfortable; his travels were lonely and his funds were chronically meager and frequently lacking completely. His diary entries often contained the ever-expressive adjective "hungry."

As he neared fifty, Hans parted with a wretchedly hot and odorous job in a St. Louis paint factory and set out for the back hills of Arkansas to homestead. He had spent long evenings in contemplation of those hills of mystery and beauty and their valleys of waiting dawn. He had read and pondered, and on occasions he had prayed.

Hans traveled by train as far as Garber Town, and from there he rode with the mail carrier to the Roark Creek Baptist Ford. The keeper of the crossroads store doubled as justice of the peace; doubled again as keeper of wills and deeds, land records and home made maps, and as the local giver of advice, also frequently outdated.

Hans pondered the advice and some of the more legible land maps. Next, in response to a rather exceptional impulse of magnanimity, he examined the gently moldering counter humidor and purchased two ten-cent cigars. He gave one to the storekeeper, retained the other for retarding anticipated hunger pains. He knew that he would be walking far before he ate again. The soda crackers that he next purchased with what remained of his quarter would serve additionally as stanchers of hunger. Having duly considered all this, Hans next used the blank side of a chewing gum poster for drafting a trail map.

So provided, the discoverer set out afoot in the latening April morning. Shadows waited as if on bended knees, and hillsides were greening and gold-dusted with new leaves. The tired old road skirted a great crescent of valley and, without benefit of a bridge or any facsimile thereof, crossed a gay young river. Hans took off his boots, carefully rolled his breeches legs to his knees, and waded the cool, fast-moving stream, watching the play of minnows that shot before him like living arrows.

When he had waded the stream and replaced and relaced his boots (Hans had never yielded to the American super-ficiality of wearing socks), he followed the road upward and westward towards the sun-splashed hills.

Before night came, the road changed to an extremely dim forest trail. The traveler stopped at a fringing of grass, built himself a cautiously small fire, and, having warmed his feet and hands, munched his crackers and smoked his cigar. Hans shed his jacket and, using it as pillow, settled himself in the open night.

By dawn he was up and again on his way. For the rest of the morning he followed the fading trail through dwarfed woods and poorland prairies of tall sedge grass still winter-brown. As the explorer would learn, the going name for it is Poor Joe Bluestem.

The trail continued to grow dimmer. Shortly after noon it almost disappeared in a far-reaching valley of bluegrass. Hans walked on until he found a footpath that people and cattle had recently walked. Within another hour he sighted a thin rising of smoke, apparently chimney smoke. A few hundred yards farther on he came to the source, a solitary log cabin deeply shaded by an oversized hedge of young cedars. An entrance was marked by remnants of an unpainted paling fence with a wide-open gateway.

Inside the cabin a woman was singing. Her voice was vibrantly young, beautifully pitched. Hans walked through the gateway and paused at the low-set side porch, which was built of split logs, faces upward. Abruptly the singing ceased. Hans viewed the heavily shadowed doorway with respectful determination. He stepped forward and knocked. Hearing no immediate answer, he knocked again and glanced into the uncurtained window. A young woman was there, but she was not answering the door; rather, she was moving away from him. But even from a brief glimpse he noted that her hair was sleek black and drawn close about her head and that a dress of blue calico hung caressingly about her exceptionally well-formed body.

But she had vanished from his sight. Hans ran a work-roughened hand through his thinning hair, turned slowly, and strolled out into the yard. Cardinals were frolicking in the haw hedges. A thrush called from a cedar tree. Hans located a yardway footpath that led around the cabin to a dark-loamed garden plot. There he saw an older woman pottering with a stub-handled hoe.

Hans spoke to her hesitantly. She put aside her hoe and momentarily leaned against the picket fence. Then she lifted the hood of her sunbonnet and peered at the newcomer, her hard, sunburned face stonily impassive. But her deep voice had a pleasant warmth. "Homesteader? Saint Looie? Well, there's passable country hereabouts. These hills—they take and they give. You figger to chop timber?"

Hans nodded. "That and farming—berries and grapes, and such things—maybe, later on, some sheep and cattle."

"How you say your name?"

"Hans Gernstacher."

"Furriner?"

"Yes, Austrian."

The garden woman studied him intently, from his gray felt hat to his closely laced, knee-length boots. Her words became more impetuous.

"I'd make you welcome to a night's lodgin', pervided you'd act neighborly tit for tat."

Hans followed her into the cabin, first scraping his boots on the sheepskin mat. The old woman brushed the hearth, laid new brushwood on the fire, untied the throat-tie of her bonnet, and hung it on a wall peg. "April nights come chilly," she noted with the emphasis of one who has come upon an astonishing truth never before surmised.

"Judy—Oh, Judy!" The old woman's lips showed the faint tracery of a smile.

Hans inquired, "It was she I heard singing?"

"Yes, Judy's my singin' purty-bird. Expect she run off when you come to the door. She's new to strangers and shy—like her pappy used to to say, like a daffydil in a risin' wind."

Hans sank into the proffered rocking chair, which creaked and sagged forebodingly. The burning hickory in the fireplace popped briskly. Colors of a beginning sunset showed at the windows. "It's later than I thought," he confided.

"Judy!"

The young woman strolled slowly into the combination living room and kitchen. She stood in the shadows beyond the woodbin, then stepped closer as Hans addressed her. "I heard you sing just now. It was very beautiful. What I mean to say is, you sing very, very well." She did not answer. She is beautiful, Hans thought, Mother of Christ, how very lovely!

"Might I hear you sing again? One of the fine old songs that, as I understand it, live hereabouts?"

The old woman slammed the cupboard door. "Sing him, Judy!" Her daughter faced the four-paned window, looked toward the brightly coloring west. She began to sing. Hans listened in wonderment. To him the song was one of daedal earth, of dancing stars, of loveliness that could never perish. She sang again and again.

The old woman was calling them to supper. Hans got to his feet, took a seat at the high round table, and viewed the meal of thin mush and heavy cream, stewed apples, hot biscuits discreetly centered with pale yellow butter, and pork souse afloat in vinegar. The caller ate lustily, and, when languor came over him, he turned to his senior hostess.

"Your daughter sings very well. She would do well with schooling——" The young woman listened eagerly. "With her good voice, her great beauty," Hans went on, "she could be made a truly great singer. Already and really, she is that."

The old woman's lips curved in a slow smile. "But that would mean sending her off to one of them college places. We're pore. All us hill folks is pore. Oftentimes the seasons ain't good to us. Thin dirt and too much rocks. Too much floods and droughts."

"It's an indebtedness to God," Hans insisted. "Your Judy's singing, I mean."

"Need her here. When young folks goes off to the town, they don't come back—hardly never do," she revised.

"I don't altogether follow you," Hans struggled for more discreet words.

"Reckon it's because you're new hereabouts. They'll shore learn you." The older woman smiled rather grimly. "They'll be plenty of time fer that, should you get yourself home-steaded."

"That will be quite soon, I hope. I've already been looking at a map. As well as I can make out, there's what they call homestead domain not far from here. Not more than seven or eight miles. . . . I begin looking tomorrow."

"Best get some rest-up first."

Hans smiled. "That's kind of you, and I'm thankful."

His counselor continued. "Better you should walk your land careful afore you stake it off. Make sure that it can be got to by autymobile, leastwise by hoss wagon."

"I agree with you. I'll look very carefully. I must have a way to town and back again."

"Hinderville 'ud come handiest fer these parts. You could get stuff hauled by truck, anyway as close in as back-totin' distance."

"I'll remember that. I'll walk on to Hinderville. As soon as I've picked my homestead and had it gone over by the government surveyor, I'll be building myself a cabin—nothing, as they say, fancy."

The old woman nodded approvingly. "Nothin' had ought to balk you out of it. Takin' time and muscle grease, a strong man like you can wrest out most of what he requires to house with—logs, rocks, chinkin' clay, all such as that. Winders and doors, and maybe some floorin' is most of all there's to be bought."

"You are right, as Americans say, like the rain. As Austrians say, like the sunshine."

"Sleep good."

"I'll be up and out early."

"I'll breakfast you out."

Still in April, Hans entered his homestead claim and established legal residence. During June he began building his cabin. It was slow building. On a pleasant south slope directly above Drake's Creek, Hans dug the cellar hole and shaped a rock foundation, tight, dry masonry without dependence on mortar. With comparatively little quarrying, he found enough smooth sandstone for shaping the walls. He hewed rafter poles and lean-to timbers from what would be his own woodlands. All his purchases together totaled little more than $150 and filled only one very light lumber truck. By mid-July he had completed his home.

Thus, Hans Gernstacher acquired the first home he had ever owned. In front of it he put a trellis which he set with morning glories and bold, gay hollyhocks. As August began, he cleared and planted a late garden which was blessed with a surprisingly generous rain. The following late afternoon, after the new settler had planted the final row of his hoped-for turnip crop, he returned to his new cabin to find a very handsome cluster of purple grapes draped above his cabin door. The grapes were delicious. Hans was certain that Judy was the donor.

Next day he made the ninety-minute walk to say thank you. He had barely arrived when Judy and her mother strolled in from their vineyard. Each carried a laundry basket heaped with the blue-black harvest. Hans complimented the harvest and spoke somewhat poetically of the reddening sunset.

The older woman appraised it matter-of-factly. "Far left it sets now, and sinks copper red. Dry, hot weather's ahead. Don't get overcropped. Feel the harsh of the grass," she added significantly.

Hans eyed her intently. "It's summer now. And not far from schooltime. I hear there is a good music and singing school down at Springfield."

"Yes," the mother nodded, "and I've most made up my mind to let Judy go to that one—startin' next month."

Hans waited in delighted amazement. "That is splendid! I can help. I still have a little money. I've spent very little."

"It won't be you that sends her. I will. But in case my little pokeful of quarter pieces runs out——"

Judy faced the west, which was by then almost blood red. She pressed a grape to her lips and smiled.

In late autumn under an infinitely blue sky, Hans set about readying a winter's supply of wood for his newly completed fireplace and bundling sumac roots for use as kindling. As he worked along through a most engaging afternoon, he heard his name called and saw his neighbor moving gingerly toward him.

"Might be you would be so kind as to read this. Hit's from Judy, and old eyes don't read so good. . . ." She held out a newly opened letter.

Hans took the letter and began to decipher the straggling handwriting, "Judy at school . . . Springfield . . . doing well . . . sings every day . . . studies every day . . . will be glad when spring comes and she can get home again. . . ." As Hans read, he felt an immense pride in Judy.

"I'm oblecged to you. Old eyes ain't fit for readin'."

That night Hans sat before his fire alone. Next morning he noticed that the farther of his two windows was traced over with frost, and the sky outside was overspread with high thin clouds.

It was a cold winter with frequent snow in January. But by late February the snow was gone. Then south winds came and with them cold, late winter rains. The rivers poured down the mountainsides in murky yellow torrents. But when the rain had ceased, the redbuds and wild cherries began to bloom, and oak trees put out their brave young leaves. Hans worked tirelessly at planting. He granted that during its first year the new land might yield stingily. But this would be an overture to a more abundant future. And by late May, Judy would be home.

On a very bright noonday she came to Hans. They walked together through a sweep of green-gold hills. With diligent reverence he gathered her a bouquet of newly arisen wildflowers. She held it to her breast and smiled happily, then placed her free hand in his. "You have helped me to go away and to come home again. You will help me . . . when my baby comes."

"I will do that."

Her hand touched his ruddy sunburned cheek. She kissed him boldly, rapturously. "Hans, let us rest here where the grass is cool and sweet. You can make love to me here in the sun. The hills . . . they will understand."

"And I will understand, too."

"He was beautiful, Hans. He was young and beautiful and strong. He was life. I am glad that I will bear his child. And I am even gladder—that you still want me."

"I understand, and I do want you."

"He was like a glorious god." Her hair glistened in the afternoon sun. Hans felt it press against his cheek. With great care she placed the bouquet of wildflowers on the young grass. For a moment she stood before him at arms' length. Then her arms closed about his waist. "You understand, Hans. And now I come to you."

"I am glad. For you are my dawn—"

They walked together through the twilight. The older woman was hoeing her garden. Judy strolled to her room. Hans walked determinedly up to her and placed his foot in the way of the hoe.

"I came to ask if I may marry Judy."

The mother studied him in steel-gray silence. She seemed very tired and almost infinitely old. "That's for you to say . . . and Judy. Whatever should you two choose together."

"The baby—her baby, it will be forever the same as my own."

Windblown leaves scurried across the path, leaves of dead years. The older woman sank her hands into the calico depths of her oversized skirt.

Autumn again. Judy singing at the churning. Falling leaves. Hans ran his fingers through his thinning and graying hair. High time he were getting back to the plowing. He already had forty acres under plow. All fenced. Nine acres planted to vineyard. A good valley of cornfield shaping up. He was now in his seventh and final year of homesteading. Hans gazed into a far acre of early November sky. Home . . . his home. Their home. By the year's end they would be owners.

The hills take and they give again. Or could it be the other way around? Hans thought of Judy's mother. Hard to believe she had passed away nearly four years before. Four times since the orchard sedge grass had been washed over with cold rains. Four springtimes had come with their wondrous flush of life. The hills take and they give again. But he had Judy. Judy with her songs, her glorious body, and her love-child son, now getting on past six. Strong, sad, beautiful. Judy would bear no other child. Hans was turned old.

He trudged into the cabin and replenished the fire. He seated himself and pressed forward to warm his feet. Too early to quit work. Hans arose and brushed the hearth. There was still work to be done before settling before the fire.

Judy was calling him to supper. He smelled frying sausage. Then he saw a shadow playing on the wall, the profile of a little boy grown grotesquely big.

BETTER FOLKS

The 1920's marked profound changes in the living sociology of the Ozarks. That decade, which some remember as the era of wonderful nonsense, saw the largest exodus of rural Ozarks population yet recorded. The United States Census Bureau's enumerations of Arkansas population began a long period of declining totals while the Missouri census remained on a plateau of relatively slight gains. For both states, and presently Oklahoma as well, the persistent exodus of rural Ozarkers from the poorer and more remote counties had much to do with lowering the respective census tallies and, in the instance of Missouri, thwarting what might have been a population increase somewhere near the national average.

The regional population statistics, of course, were destined to endure continuing changes. The subsequent population declines of Arkansas and Oklahoma were to be accentuated by the regrettable losses of Negro citizens, in great part sharecroppers and tenant farmers, who found themselves being intolerably repressed and pauperized by a now perennial agricultural depression. The cumulative futility and collapse of poor-land cotton growing proved to be the ultimate stinger to the Negro sharecroppers who had endured as distressed country neighbors.

However, even for the landowning farmers or yeomen, the 1920's placed the Ozarks economy under extreme and imperiling strain. Throughout the nation the survival of subsistence agriculture and the family farm, to which the Ozarks had contributed importantly, was in very deep trouble. At the time the Ozarks had comparatively few alleviating industries. These few, which included commercial canneries, hardwood sawmills, and poultry-processing plants were preponderantly small and inadequate to stabilize or bail out the poverty-dogged agriculture. Long before the 1920's came to an end, the Ozarks at large were being strafed by and in great areas quite literally engulfed in poverty.

This was destined to linger. The town labor markets, traditionally under par if not penny whistle, continued to limp and lag. It followed that, however admirable the living partnership of rural people and their land and rain and sunshine, the rural Ozarks were very seriously impeded in terms of earning livelihoods and living from season to season.

Granting it had never been high enough to skid spectacularly, the lowering economy of the rural Ozarkers was hurting the validity of their culture, including their long distinctive wealth of tellin' stories. For profoundly human reasons the era of taller, more imaginative yarns was dimming. The rifts between towns and their countrysides were widening and deepening. In more and more instances the tellin' stories were being pegged on the lean-as-a-red-rooster, poor-as-Job's-turkey, or, as some put it, cornpone-and-branch-water hard times of the rural Ozarkers. The tellin' stories grew less imaginative and more strongly rooted in the mundane encroachments of poverty.

The failing or faltering Ozarks fortunes of the 1920's were further darkened and complicated by the catastrophic depression of the 1930's. These muddyings, so it seems to me, were intensified by the practices of such self-perpetuating rashes as the town-based Chambers of Commerce that began to impose a persistent palaver of evasion and distortion. The imposition, here, was based more on evading the facts than falsifying them. Their coming, however, was nevertheless regrettably toxic to indigenous expression. The town-propagated "C of C" grew epidemic during the 1920's, insidious during the 1930's, and openly obnoxious during the advent of the inflationary war economy of the tragic 1940's. As a counter-irritant to the Chamber of Commerce there arose a hat-passing organization known as the Ozarks Playground Association with the specious slogan, *Ozarks: Land of a Million Smiles.*

The redeeming truth is that despite these lingering distempers and the deplorable misfortunes of the principal source of livelihood, farming, the Ozarks as a widely spread whole have retained their indigenous integrity.

This story speaks best for itself. It was a local tellin' story of the 1920's, a spoken chronicle of real Ozarks people who stood valiantly, even if less than triumphantly, against forces that would destroy them.

CHARLIE and Mame Tatum were Arkansas woodcutters. They were good woodcutters, too, considering how the odds stood against them. Mame was scrawny and bent and predisposed to chest miseries. Charlie was lacking an arm. But even Squire Leander Trent, veteran of sixty-eight years of sustained thrift, admitted that the old couple were first-rate woodcutters. The Squire had good reason to know; off and on for twenty-two years, good old Leander had been hiring the white-trash Tatums to clear building lots of excessive trees and paying them a dollar a rick or a dollar and a half a cord to saw and chop the waste wood into marketable stove or fireplace fuel. The prevailing rate for chopping was at least a quarter dollar a rick or a half dollar a cord higher. But the going practice was to hire reasonably able-bodied men—not stove-up half-cripples.

The time-battered couple were close cutters. They would chop up twigs no thicker than your thumb, and they could split the roughest of knots and stump cuts into heater chunks. Moreover, they stacked their wood in full-measured ricks or cords and played no tricks in stacking it. Mame was the honest member of the firm. It was she who discouraged Charlie's making use of shady methods of stacking. On the other hand, Charlie was the more industrious member. With vehemence he encouraged Mame to avoid the sweet elysium of loiter.

And any way you sized him, and granting, as one had to, that he was lacking a right arm and hand, Charlie Tatum was no weakling. And he was no pamperer of women, the less so because Mame had a part in costing him his right arm.

The untoward parting took place one night when Charlie was discussing the advantages of travel with an uninvited guest. It is true that he was waving a double-bladed ax for purposes of emphasis; also that the caller had not come by merely to visit with Charlie.

Lyin' Whiff Whitfield had a scad of talents; he could scream like an eagle, caw like a crow, dance a fast jig, bray like a jackass, crow like a bantam rooster, squeak like a trapped rat, and pull off bottle caps with his front teeth. And he could draw the women like a molasses barrel draws flies.

What Charlie Tatum didn't know was that Lyin' Whiff Whitfield was also an accomplished axman; further, that he didn't take to being used as a chopping block. It followed that when Charlie began waving the big ax at him, Whiff Whitfield grabbed up Mame's lighter, double-bitted ax from beside the doorsill. It was an undersize tool but at least as sharp as an undertaker's razor.

Right about there Charlie Tatum lost his temper and, a split second later his right arm. When he charged Lyin' Whiff, the ladies' comforter paused long enough to throw the lighter ax. It cut deep into Charlie's right arm, just below the biceps. It didn't quite sever the bone, but Doc Hatchcock did as soon as he got there.

The year before she joined up with Charlie, Mame had borne a man-child whom she named Henry without openly specifying a surname. There were those who represented that little Henry was an aftermath of the late August revival meeting and brush arbor over at Panther Scald crossroads. But at very least, Henry was a real pretty baby, and, as Mame stated, there are people who would tripe-hang the Almighty Hisself.

Charlie's accident made a lot of difference. It kept him out of work for almost two years, and, as Mame perceptively noted, it bittered him up something awful. Among principal victims was little Henry, who was just turning five at the time of the accident. Granting that the child was fairly healthy and certainly no more devilish than the run of brats of his age, Mame's Henry didn't stay around Charlie much longer. For all peeves and pooh-poohing aside, was Charlie Tatum, now bad crippled, supposed to feed and shelter a brat not of his own flesh? "Hell no" is as easily said as "hell yes." Besides, the brat was able-bodied. In a few more years he'd be big enough to start filling his own gut. On the more benevolent side, Charlie had a half cousin known as Stinker Covington. Anyway, Cousin Covington kept a peckerwood sawmill and five young boys of his own. One more wouldn't make no great difference, and pretty soon it would give him another log lifter.

Mame didn't say much, but she took parting with her baby boy real hard. She appeared to age about fifteen years in that many days. But just the same, she stayed on with Charlie, nursed him, and, when his stub finally got healed over, she went with him back to chopping wood.

It was cruel hard. De-arming a man unbalances his ax work and a lot besides. They got so rock-bottom poor they had to give up the two-room-and-lean-to house they had been renting from Homer Leathers and take over what used to be the weighing shack out beyond the canning factory's hog lot.

Pickings were mighty lean for another year. But the couple tided through another winter by chopping, and come spring and summer they picked strawberries, planted garden patches, stacked wheat and oats, harvested beans and tomatoes and sweet potatoes, picked up windfall apples, and in the fall helped out with hog killings and built fences. That went on for about seventeen years following Charlie's accident, and, as the years dallied along, Mame got more and more dour and spleeny. But Charlie didn't wax fat, either. His once bulgy cheeks puckered and sunburned to the red of a seedling apple. He began to develop internal pains and rumblings, which according to Doc Hatchcock represented the delayed vengeance of youthful wild oats. Mame offered prayer, Charlie denials.

But came another winter there was still more aggravation. They had set to clearing the timber from the site of some of Squire Trent's would-be building lots. While propping a heavy log for crosscut sawing, Mame strained too hard at the tip of the pry-pole. She felt a snap somewhere deep in her ailing chest and collapsed.

Charlie cajoled and cursed and, finding neither of any avail, inveigled the help of two plumber's assistants to carry the fainting woman back to the shack. For three days Mame writhed with high fever. Then she lay for long hours in a dark stupor from which she finally awoke cold and colorless but strangely alert. Charlie was worried. He had lost the helpfulness of his work partner; he was roped into a nursing job, which was commencing to look like maybe it would turn out to be a buryin'. Furthermore, the mantelboard cigar box where he kept his money was beginning to show bare spaces on the bottom.

Next day a peddler came; a round-faced, blue-eyed, gangling youth, ill at ease and awkward, but withal clean-featured and likable-looking. Overlooking the formality of waiting to be asked in, he entered with a nervous "Good mawnin'," unhooked his sample bag and opened it to display an extensive assortment of medicines, herbs, soaps, powders, tablets, extracts, pills, tonics, and bath salts—all in bright-colored wrappers with green printing.

One-armed Charlie favored forcefully encouraging the caller's exit. He had no hard-earned money to waste on silly knickknacks for a grunty old woman who, any fool could see, would be better off at work.

Mame readjusted the mildewed quilt and slipped a trifle closer to the boy. "An' how old be ye?"

"Goin' on twenty-two, ma'am. This yeller powder here is figgered and sot to make a dead 'un well. Ole Doc Tannihill over at Hindsville, he says he's been a-peddlin' remedies for better'n fawty year, and he says he ain't never saw nothin' like it yit. Lemme tell you about the formiler. Here 'tis in plain writin' but I'll read it fer ye——'

"Say ye be twenty-two?"

"Goin' on twenty-two. It reads here on the wrapper——"

"Where's ye raised at?"

The youth mopped his forehead with an extensive blue-speckled handkerchief. "I was sort of a orphling. Borned down about Red Star. Ever been thereaways?"

"I reckon mebbe I have."

"Course ye have," Charlie interceded surlily. "Lived thar half your lifetime."

The peddler continued diffidently. "I ain't able to recollect no great amount. But I got borned and started by my ma, and after that I got partly raised by Ole Stinky Joe Covington and put out to loggin' from Panther Scald. Then Stinky Joe wist me off as hired boy to Jedge Dowell down by Weddington Gap. I growed up thereabouts. And now I'm tryin' for to get ahead." He paused as if waiting encouragement that was not forthcoming. Charlie Tatum was no talk-maker, and Mame only asked questions.

"What be you aim to do next?"

"I-I'm goin' to git married."

The peddler stopped short. Mame lay strangely still and pale as a flour sack.

"She ain't been gettin' no exercise," Charlie's voice bore a complacency that his actions did not substantiate. He shook his spouse and slapped her shoulders. Mame stirred and blinked, whereupon the new fledged vendor continued in tones of revived confidence. "So I'm doin' a little peddlin' to git started on. Buy a few home fixin's, maybe a plow, and gard'nin' tools, one thing 'nother like folks needs when they're new-married."

"An' who might the gal be?" Mame asked.

"Ain't much chance you'd know her. Name's Lulu Combs, ol' Ike Combs' gal. Yes, ye see, ol' Ike, he says he'd tenant us a thirty-acre plantin' patch, an' give us the loan of a team of hosses an' a turnin' plow. I got to buy a bull-tongue plow, but he'll leave us have a shack to live in. So I'm doin' some peddlin' to git started off on."

Mame lay still. A tear rolled down her cheek like a trickle of cold spring water. Charlie was mumbling half-audible dictums to the effect that no such money-burning monkey-shines as peddler's junk were to be brought into his house so long as he was conscious and able. He spat and glanced meaningfully toward the door.

But for once Mame erred from his masterful judgment. "Say them yeller powders is good for chist pains?"

"Chist pains, headache, y'earache, lumbago, rheumatiz-swelled-up j'ints, and all sich cawnditions."

"S'pose ye gimme 'bout three a them bottles of the yeller."

"That'll be six bits."

"All right, all right. Charlie, git the lad three quarters out from my berry-pickin' money in the cracked teacup in the seegar box in the top drawer that washbowl stand."

Charlie Tatum took an uncertain step backwards, his fist clenched, his lips clamped tight, and he strove for words. Such defiance within his own household was heretofore unknown. Then Mame added, "Nev' mind, nev' mind. You can git it yourse'f, Honey. Right thar in the old teacup."

Charlie moved to toss the peddler out the front door. But he hesitated, and, during that interval, the young peddler pocketed the three quarters, promised that he would come again on the morrow, left the medicine, and headed for the door. And Mame was fallen back again whiter than a flour-barrel ghost. Charlie saw nothing to do but grin and bear it, granting there was no sensible cause for grinning.

He trudged outside into a bristling autumn morning, down the sedge-grass lane toward the timber clearing. Dead leaves whirled windblown as if spilled from the gray, puckered clouds. Charlie continued staunchly and arrived at the lot. He yanked off his overalls jacket and let the wind make through the tatters of his shirt.

Then he singled out a strong-bodied red oak, thumped at its butt with his ax, stepped back, and surveyed its bared forest of limbs. To fell such a tree would offer a considerable problem even to a two-armed ax man, for its body was straight as a flagstaff and its limbs distributed with such symmetry and balance that neither side promised a pound of vantage in pull.

Charlie spat and pondered. The tree was a ninepin—a natural balance. Cut with an ax, there would be virtually no telling which way the oak might choose to fall. Of course, with a power saw, or even a two-man crosscut, a feller could shape a down cut and drive a glut and a couple of wedges. But, hell, he didn't have a power saw. He didn't have a partner in shape to help pull a crosscut. And he didn't have wedges or gluts or a mallet. But he did have a good ax and one good arm.

It meant a hard job, but Charlie wasn't daunted. Life had deluged him with hard jobs. Now he was at a place where only a hard job could soothe him. He wanted to do more than chop a tree. He wanted to chop the tallest and fattest and firmest-set tree on the whole damn lot. For sure, Charlie Tatum was not the man to be put to fright by any damn six-rick red oak. Of course, if Mame were along, they could have sawed down a sharp slope cut, chopped a deep nick on the other side and over the tree would go—in whatever direction he wanted it to fall.

All at once the burden of singleness weighed heavily. Even so, Charlie spat on the sharper edge of his ax and swung valiantly to outline a first chip row. He would make it a foot wide and deepen to eighteen inches. That would be close to half the trunk's thickness.

The pungent odor of fresh sapwood, the spanking crack of his ax, the whine of far-flung chips provided a satisfying feeling of mastery. The splattering of chips increased, and the cut deepened until now the point of his ax bit into the year-circled heart of the tree. Then the wedge-shaped notch came to a point.

Charlie rested for a time, leaning upon the handle of his ax, panting, and issuing joyous execrations at the hardness of the wood. Then he sauntered to the other side of the tree and began to chop again. The swing and recoil of the heavy ax tugged hard at his unsupported arm. The whipping wind brought water to his eyes. Time after time he paused, sobbing for breath.

But this Tatum was not a man to be worn down by any

tree. He landed a deluging shower of blows and deepened the notch until the trunk lacked less than an inch of being cut clear of its stump. For half an hour he hacked out small chips and ax shavings, but the big tree stood firm.

Charlie raised the head of his ax, shoved it against the body of the oak, and pushed with all his might. But the big tree stood firm as a mountain. He spat on his hand, grasped the ax again, and, flattening the arch of its swing, landed a dozen more good licks. Light shone through the white sapwood, but still the oak stood like a giant ninepin.

The one-armed man lifted his ax again, rammed the bit of it against the tree's trunk and shoved with all his might. For a split second it seemed that the oak would topple before his frenzied boosts. But the fragment of uncut heartwood held. Again the oak came to a treacherous balance, as if steadied by a mighty, unseen hand. Charlie cursed at the satanic line of uncut hardwood. But the damned tree just stood there.

It was defying the chopper.

Whatever defied Charlie Tatum had another lesson to learn. Mame had learned. Grown up or not, Mame's brat would learn. All of them would learn that even if old Charlie was poor and bedraggled and generally bedamned, in the one little way that was left him he would do the telling. Or else. He swung again with his ax. The huge body of the oak quivered ever so slightly. Charlie chopped again and again, and the recoil of the ax handle jarred and burned his hand. Then he paused for breath. A light fantasy of wind played high among the tips of the tallest branches. The one-armer grabbed the tip of the ax handle and again charged at the body of the tree. There was a cracking snap. Then he felt an overpowering pressure against the head of his ax. He sobbed, swore, and pushed again.

The big tree was choosing to fall the wrong way. With only two possible directions to tumble in, the damned old oak was choosing the contrary way. It would smash a fence if it did. But that wasn't the real point. He could build back a fence. The point was that no tree ever had fallen contrary to Charlie Tatum and his ax. He had brought down thousands of trees —felled them the way he wanted them to fall.

But now all the force of the universe seemed to be hurling itself against the head of his ax. He stamped frantically to shape a foothold. And as the tree pressed still harder against his axhead, Charlie pushed again to the last ounce and dreg of his strength.

Then all in a split second the mighty body of the tree began twisting clear of the stump and siding in just the way he intended that it shouldn't. Charlie held like a prop of iron. He became aware of strange shapes above his head. Splotches of red played before his eyes. When a big tree totters, one hard push can swerve a mighty lot of weight. So Charlie pushed hard once more. Then he tried frantically to leap clear. But the tree was closing down on him, cracking and swishing and smashing. He felt a stupefying impact of vast and unimaginable weight.

Then he lay still, looking up into a sweep of autumn clouds. He was tired, so very tired. The smell of leaves was sweet and the damp black soil softer than a rich man's featherbed. Hurt? Hurt? Maybe so. But mainly he was sleepy, too sleepy to really care. Might have caught a glancing blow on the head. Maybe his chest was smashed in. What did it matter? At least the damned big tree wasn't exactly on top of him. At least he had brought it to earth. And so he lay motionless, half-smiling.

Mame spent the afternoon in a slow, soggy kind of doze.

From time to time the invading sunlight marked the image of a face, the face of a young man, trusting, wide-eyed, glad about life. The remedy peddler. Mame's hand went to her breast. Her son. Her baby boy.

The richness of the slanting sunlight came upon her again. The wind brought to her the odor of fresh black soil, and perfumes of flowers long forgotten. Then the shadows became thin and long, and the cold night winds came. Mame slept.

When she awoke it was daybreak. The air was caressing, soft as the flesh of a new-born baby, and the colors of dawn were at her window. By midmorning the remedy peddler was there again, amiable and grinning.

"How'd ye find them powders, ma'am?"

"They done me good, boy, they done me good. Maybe ye got somethin' jest a wee bit stronger?"

"Oh, yes, ma'am. I got lots of pain-easin' pills . . . big ones. First-rate fer chist pains and gallopin' headaches. Jest two's a dose. More'n four is dange-russ. Doc Tannihill says as how six of 'em would kill a span of loggin' mules."

"What be they worth?"

"Four bits a bottle."

"How many bottles ye got?"

"Eight bottles."

"Gimme all them bottles."

"Lemme see, that there'll be . . . eight times ought is ought, eight fives is . . . That'd be four dollars evun."

"Well, Honey, you look in that ole seegar box on the mantel-board. Take *all* the money they is in it."

The medicine seller hastened to comply. "But, sa-ay, Missus! They's—lemme count! They's twenty-one dollars and a quarter in this here teacup."

"Take it, boy, take it all!"

"I-I don't onderstand ye, ma'am."

"Take it all. You an' the gal will be needin' hit fer startin' out new-married—"

"Oh? Thank ye, ma'am! I'll leave all these here tablets here beside ye. Much obliged!"

"You an' her'll build up good lives. . . ."

"Yes ma'am."

"You'll be a good man an' stand up fer your own. . . ."

"Yes ma'am."

"You-all will be strong where we was weak. . . ."

"Yes ma'am."

"You'll make for better folks. . . ."

The remedy peddler took leave in an evidently joyous haze. But before he was well out of sight, Mame had put to test the curing capacity of her purchase. One after another she swallowed twelve of the tablets.

MORE LIGHT

As the 1920's began, the mood, material, and spirit of Ozarks tellin' stories had been in mutation for the greater part of a century. As the 1920's came to an end, Ozarks tellin' stories were beginning to fade—like hill-country rainbows in the still implicitly beautiful throes of meeting the sunset.

Throughout earlier generations of Ozarks settlement, the tellin' stories had found their borning and most of their usefulness in the realities of exceptional remoteness. Their advantages included the persisting scarcity of literacy and a counterbalancing abundance of intelligent and imaginative country people with the time for telling and for listening. Even so, and for convincingly human causes, the gists of the stories persistently changed. Gradually the recountings of frontier adventures were replaced by accounts of goings and comings and the travails of impoverished people who faced forces of torment or destruction.

During the early 1900's the tellin' stories began to reach, or at least to look, farther beyond home boundaries. In so doing they began to shape or indicate increasing acquaintance with the printed word. Even so the printed word infiltrated slowly or tardily, as did the attainability of public education. For purposes of vetting this point, which seems to me absolutely basic, the writer may be forgiven for briefly indulging in an old man's urge to reminisce.

Back in 1890 my mother, who grew up in a fairly typical back-hill Ozarks community still known as Hog Eye (It is in one of the less-heeded fringes of Washington County), became the first woman to receive a bachelor's degree from the then mewling University of Arkansas. She was twenty-four at the time. She had grown up in a community where no school had ever "kept" longer than eight weeks a year or "carried" beyond the fourth grade. Mother recalled having been "turned back in arithmetic" three times because none of the teachers knew how to "do" fractions.

When she was fifteen, my mother was taken in by gracious kinfolk at Fayetteville and given an opportunity to attend the "preparatory department," which at the time held about two-thirds of the enrollment of the leading university within the Ozarks region. After five years in "Preparatory," my mother worked on to win her degree; she was the only woman and the youngest member of a graduating class of six. My father, by contrast, never attended public school; his total schooling included about three years in private academies.

Schooling in Fayetteville, Arkansas, has long been far above the prevailing Ozarks averages. Even so, in 1922, when I was graduated from the Fayetteville high school, the class valedictorian stated with feeling and evident sincerity that she and her fellow graduates were then prepared to go home and read the newspapers to our parents.

My high school graduating class had forty-eight members, twenty-six from the town and twenty-two from nearby rural communities. That fewer than half of the parents of the graduates were then able to read newspapers was a reasonable deduction. Four years later three members of my graduating class at the University of Arkansas could claim the distinction of being the first college graduates from their respective Ozarks counties. By then (1926), the University of Arkansas was far and away the best accredited college in the so-called true Ozarks. But the lingering scarcity of high school graduates in the state held down its enrollment to fewer than a thousand students.

The relevancy of the foregoing to the birth, growth, and decline of the Ozarks tellin' stories seems at least dimly evident.

In considerable part because schooling was exceptionally belated so was the inevitable fading of the Ozarks tellin' story.

The temporary close-out of the gargantuan brawl which Franklin Roosevelt dubbed "the Global War" saw impressive gains in public education throughout most of the Ozarks. This was attained largely by way of consolidated schools in many rural areas. For better or worse, as public education moved in and up, the tellin' stories receded.

About here an insertion seems to raise its noisy head. The coming of radio, beginning with battery-powered crystal sets, began during the latter 1920's. It gained formidably during the 1930's, and, with the augmented power-line era which reached a humming crescendo late in the 1940's, radio continued to shape up as an invincible tide of mass communication.

Radio could talk, God forbid, without need or place for direct answers or assembled audiences. Around the clock and calendar radio set up its unrelenting deluges of talk, "music," or remotely musical noise, hawking, hoaxing, and news broadcasts. Its reach and penetration were and still are wholly unprecedented and practically invincible. In terms of commandable attention radio keeps on outdistancing all the other communications media, not excepting its monster offspring, television.

Abetted by the enticement of words pouring from invisible mouths and multitudes of other noises without visible sources, radio begot and holds to the almost fiendishly compulsive resource of luring the listener by whetting, massaging, or "channeling" his curiosity. As implicit evidence of this attainment, radio redounds and deluges with spits of tellin' stories that however deplorable are able to command our attention. During its so-called golden age, radio hawked and squawked with every known manner of storied invention and innovation—adventure stories, crime stories, sex stories, grimly designed funny stories, and so on by the night and day. Wherever its locale or whatever its text, the tellin' story was being literally counter-noised into extinction. Isolation and solitude were and, alas, still are being murdered.

One is therefore compelled to grant that radio helped formidably to bring about the final if somewhat befogged twilight of the Ozarks tellin' story.

But the issue of schooling nevertheless remained at root levels. During the early 1920's many rural Ozarkers set about pondering in their own words and experiences what many saw vividly as the cross furrows of "natural living" and "educated living."

What follows is one onlooker's and inlistener's attempt to reduce to print one such recounting which is reasonably typical of many. What follows, as I see and feel it, is punctuated by the figurative death rattle of the Ozarks tellin' story.

IT began back in Jasper, Arkansas, when Rufus Sloane won a place as alternate on the high school debating team. There were several who doubted that Jasper had a real high school; in time none could honestly doubt that J.H.S., or call it what one chose to, had a real debating team. Rufus Sloane saw to that. After the first affirmative got sent up for cattle stealing, Alternate Sloane made the home-town debating team a real humdinger.

Graduation evenin' found the same Rufus class valedictorian. He spoke for forty-two minutes on "The History and Progress of Scandinavian Immigration Since 1851." The audience somehow endured it; only three left the "hosting" First Baptist Church before the oration was finished. One was the Baptist preacher, who couldn't sit on account of his rose rash; the second was Miss Lila Rolston, the English teacher with thirty-minute kidneys; the other was old Brun Wilson, who just couldn't hold out longer than half an hour without a drink. (Only two Sundays before while Parson Bullthropps was lining out the hymn, "I Need Thee Every Hour," Brun was overheard to say, "Hell, Parson, I need *three* every hour.")

By the time he had finished off his valedictory, most probably long before, Rufus had made his climaxing decision. He was going to college. His father, rather widely known as "Sour Bill" Sloane, the railroad crosstie buyer, had earlier reached a contrary decision. His son, Rufus, was going to grow up to be a sensible, country-style Democrat politician, like Pappy Faubus over on Greasy Creek.

That night after the Sloane home was permeated with Bill's honest snoring, Effie Sloane and her only son, Rufus, held a hushed but determined conference in the kitchen. Rufus was annoyed by an excessive moistening of the eye. Mrs. Sloane's lips quivered as she recounted her husband's selfishness and stinginess. The fact remained that when last faced squarely with the question of Rufus's future, Bill Sloane had almost roared, "Send that young lunkhead to college! Hell, no! I ain't a-goin' to do it!"

Effie was going to do it, at very least she was going to help do it. Abused wife that she was, Effie had determination, two one-hundred-dollar Liberty Bonds, a gen-uwine lady's gold wristwatch, six shares in the Elkins Cannery inherited from her first husband, and ways of making still more money, such as baking and selling fruit cakes. Her only son Rufus was going to college; he was going to get ahead in the world.

It followed that September 24, 1922, found Rufus in a brand-new $19.95 suit, guaranteed to be appropriate for college wear, a pair of $2.95 yellow-tan, low-quarter shoes, a red-striped $2.45 silk shirt, and carrying an imitation leather accordion handbag, $6.95. He was embarking for Fayetteville on a two-coach, Missouri–North Arkansas train, minimum rates. He was setting out with a distinctly cool paternal farewell, $213.50 in cash, a pair of burning eyelids, and a feeling of intense nausea. On arrival at the squat, foul-smelling depot at Fayetteville, Arkansas, Rufus alighted from the train and walked westward until he was temporarily assigned a second-floor room in an appallingly ugly dormitory where he was asleep before he had surely located the light.

By eight that evening the University of Arkansas Student Activities and Conduct Council and Christian Youth Conference were in intensive session. In attendance were the pastors of the nine Protestant churches of the town, eleven students representing their respective fraternities, three more representatives of the dormitories, and one extremely bilious-looking youth who confessed that he represented "town" students; also, seven senior faculty members. Fluency was enhanced by a gratis half-bushel of extremely juicy Winesap apples contributed by the Academic Committee of the local Rotary Club.

As an opener, the student president of the Y.M.C.A. offered a hard-breathing exhortation to row for a winning gospel team while rooting for a winning football team. Next up was the Dean of Men who had lately ravaged a very large ham dinner at the Pho Nu House. Having hooded his protruding belly with his gray flannel jacket, Dean Emmett Ripley wiped his hands and fell to, speaking in an appallingly shrill, puerile voice.

". . . Gentlemen, you can never make men perfect. If college boys weren't a little rough, a little boisterous, and a little indiscreet at times, they wouldn't be college boys. I—I was a college boy once myself—" His voice quavered. "I'm a boy yet—a little fat, a little gray, I grant you—but a boy all the same. In my work I try to feel for the boys, live with the boys; that is, I—ah, live *for* the boys."

A sustained hush. "I say, gentlemen, let boys be boys, because of all the puzzling and wonderful creatures in the world, I believe an eighteen-year-old boy the most mostest. But with all this, I trust my son Kendricks there"—pointing to a pale, goggled youngster—"I trust my son Kendricks as completely as I trust myself."

The Dean accepted a handful of the small juicy apples and bowed to vehement applause.

Next up to speak was Dr. Virgil L. Hancock, head of the English department and for twenty-five years a faithful church worker and a dutiful, conscientious teacher. He opened with a forthright plea that his fellow teachers and church workers rededicate themselves to "restraining academic barbarity."

The Reverend M. Gillespie Wilbanks sought to conclude the program fittingly—he prayed and prayed and prayed. He prayed for the prosperity of his great church, for the progress of the students who regularly attended the services of his great church, and even for those who faithfully attended services of other great churches. He exhorted a stern and ever-observant Jehovah to stamp out radicalism and debauchery and infidelism in the University with boots amply spiked. He prayed that the young men and women of the great commonwealth of Arkansas would shape themselves into substantial cobblestones for use in paving the way of the Lord.

"Felwahs," Y.M.C.A. secretary Megson began, "it's up to every one of us to put into life these wonderful thoughts and deeds and messages that these worthy, wonderful men have spoken this evening. . . . There are nearly thirty sandwiches and a panful of fruit salad waiting for us to clean up."

The cleaning-up was attained promptly and vigorously. Coats and hats were donned with bustling piety. The uplift workers filed forth into the mildly chilly night. Next day was registration. The day following was class opening.

Morning came with a clanging of hour bells, a banging upstairs, embarrassing collisions coming downstairs, hand-shaking, backslapping, jollying, scamperings, and loafing. Rufus paced the lower hall of the Main Building, awesomely conscious of its garnishment of loungers who were better dressed than he. He entered a well-filled room presided over by a nervous little man who was attempting to pronounce his students' names.

"Now, this heah-ah course is human ah-geography-uh. I— mean to review this mornin' ah—on Simple's ah-principle of the influences of ah-geographical uh-environment—"

Rufus listened in benumbing boredom, attempting to amuse himself by counting the "ahs" and "uhs."

"Ah, Mr. Sloane—— *Who* is Mr. Sloane?"

Rufus stiffened alertly and raised his hand.

"Mr. Sloane, uh-what makes the wind blow?"

"Why—" A finger snapped tormentingly behind his ear.

"All right, the young lady uh-behind Mr. Sloane—your name?"

"Jeannette Akin."

"Miss Akin, uh-what makes the wind blow?"

"God!"

Rufus laughed, to his own surprise, rather loudly.

"Oh, now, Mr. uh-Sloane, what complex do you suffer under? Miss Akin is uh-right, I am sure, but-uh I had reference to the scientific cause."

"Is it change in pressure?"

"Exactly. Uh, who spoke? Let us leave the thought for the next lesson. Uh, class dismissed!"

Psychology followed—in Room 16, Main Hall. Rufus arrived at the door just as it was being methodically closed by a gray-haired, plastery-complexioned little man who appeared badly lost in a loose-fitting and extremely shiny blue serge suit.

"Come on in, sir, and take that second seat in the third row, please—— No, not that one—the one next it. Yes, now will everyone be seated, if you please, and next we will—now, I asked you once to leave those chairs in the same position that you found them in. I have a reason for having them kept that way. Mr. Hapsman—Mr. Moxie—or it is Mr. Sloane? Will you please face to the front? Now, everyone! Your attention here on the blackboard, please!

"Now, everyone! What is the definition of psychology?"

A finger-snapping hand arose.

"Yes, sir, all right, sir, what is your definition?"

"Well—psychology is ah—the science which aims to hitch up the human mind with the human soul—ah, I think."

"Well sir, yes sir—— Is there another definition?"

A shrilly penetrating voice came forth, "I ain't got no definition, but I want to ask now if evolution is going to be upheld in this here course? I'm a-askin' because I'm a minister of the Gospel of the livin' Jesus Christ, and I'd like to know pretty early——"

"Yes sir, yes sir, as a rule we make a special effort to steer clear of the issue of evolution in this course—and to continue —your attention here, please! We are looking for the facts of the case. Does anyone know the facts of the case already?"

"Whut case?" The question was put by a slightly worse-for-the-wear, cotton-gin ex-pugilist from the delta country.

"Take out your Seashores, please!"

Here, knowing winks were exchanged between two Percheron-dimensioned football players and a student-about-town soak. The trio were draped over chairs in the rear corner of the room.

"Seashore—Seashore's *Experiments in Psychology*. I believe I have mentioned the work before——"

"It ain't been mentioned yit," a complacent, gum-chewing, freckled girl in the front row volunteered.

"Very well, you will purchase—"

There followed a freshman military art class under Lieutenant Bueret Bolster, U.S.A. Rufus had been drafted into the course by authority of the military training compulsion whereby all male freshmen and sophomore students were required to take two years of military training.

"Abshire, what does a man owe his country in case of war? Stand up!"

"Well, he ought to serve in the army in case of war."

"Right sir! What woulda happened to us in the last war if we hadn't had no army—Sloane!"

Competition was sharp of tooth and claw. A serious, sharp-featured youth on the front row usurped Rufus' materializing response. He burst forth, "We'd a-been wiped off'n the face of the earth, suh!"

"That's just ejackly right, sir!" the lieutenant instructor shouted. "Now, we won't have no lesson this morning, only I would like to tell you men to be sure to get yourselves to drill every Monday and Thursday afternoon, and while you are drilling or listening to class work, to keep on the alert and honor the uniform. . . . Desmissed!"

Next on Rufus' schedule came freshman physics. By time for the hour gong the front entrance of the two-story gray frame building labeled Physics Hall was somewhat confusedly littered with firstcomers. Several minutes after the gong the door flew open as if from violent concussion within, and an objectionably shrill voice piped, "Come right on in, people, right on in! Get your hands out of your pockets and come right on in and find yourselves seats. You fellows leaning against the water spout, come on in! Don't be bashful! Now sit down—now sa-a-y, there's no law prohibiting a person's sitting on the front row in here, and remember, now, that in this class a student's grade is just as likely as not to vary directly as the square of the distance from his seat to the teacher's desk."

The instructor laughed appreciatively. "My name is Ripley—Emmett Ripley. I am also dean of men, too. So you see, I have lots of puzzling things to deal with."

"Now, sit down—sit down! . . . Mr. Kile!"

"Heah," a back-row voice ventured weakly. The dean-instructor ceased swabbing his coat and fixed his pale blue eyes inquiringly upon the luckless Mr. Kile.

"Kile, there is a glass full of water on my desk. How does that glass differ from an ordinary glass?"

Kile meditated solemnly, then shook his head resignedly.

"Why, you—you—" the Dean's double chin quavered in anticipation. "Kile, you move your head crossways when you ought to move it up and down. The glass of water is different from the ordinary glass because it is full of water."

The good Dean slapped his knees, elevated his chin, and divulged three rapid-fire guffaws in regularly diminishing staccato. In time the class also laughed. In due course the instructor-comedian returned to his role as senior educator and philosopher. Pushing his hands into his pockets, Emmett Ripley gazed intently at the ceiling and continued to shrill.

"The world is full of narrow men, narrow minds, and narrow niches; but I am not narrow. I don't have any little idols on top of my mantel; in fact, I want to tell you right here, the first morning of this course, that if anyone here thinks I am wrong at any time and can prove it to me, I am ready to listen to what he has to say. But mind you, you have to prove your point to me because I am out for the facts, and I'll tell you right here that I'd barter my chances for Paradise to add to the number of known facts.

"When the facts are known, we learn that nature is kind

and science is kind and both are fair; they borrow and return —borrow and return. Now it may be that when you were children you had a pet cat, maybe, and the cat died, and you held a little funeral for the kitty, maybe, out behind the barn where nobody would see you, and you buried the kitty out in the garden, maybe, and forgot all about it.

"Well, h-r-rump . . . and the next spring your father plowed the garden, and maybe it just happened that he planted radishes where the kitty was buried, and you ate the radishes, and they were all the sweeter because the kitty had been there. And you had forgotten all about the kitty, and, um-m-m-m, those radishes were *good*! Oh yes, nature *is* kind.

"Well, I won't ask you anything today, because I don't think you know much to say, because the first day I went to college I didn't know much, and I did hope the teacher wouldn't call on me. And he didn't the first day, so I won't ask you anything at this time. Next Wednesday we will take Lesson One."

His classes finished for the day, Rufus made for the dormitory in anticipation of supper. The oak leaves were falling as a pack of stray dogs swept past him in rather riotous preoccupation with canine sex relations. A frowzy youngster in a red sweater was standing out on the front balcony rendering a shrilly whistled interpretation of "It's a Long, Long Way to Tipperary."

Rufus looked down at the drought-seared grass and the tired, browning oak leaves. "I can't stand it here, and I can't go home. What the hell am I goin' to do?"

The paper on which this book is printed bears the watermark of the University of Oklahoma Press and has an effective life of at least three hundred years.